AT LAST I KNEW
WHAT I HAD TO DO . . .

I stood there—holding on to my memories, my love for that house. A place they called ugly. My memories knew better. The house was beautiful.

I made my way back to the house and got into bed. As I lay there, how full the house was. How full was I! "You're not dead!" I kept telling the house. "I won't let them do it. And I'll make them remember too. I promise."

A Place Called Ugly

AVI

AN AVON  FLARE BOOK

AVON BOOKS, INC.
1350 Avenue of the Americas
New York, New York 10019

Copyright © 1981 by Avi Wortis
Published by arrangement with McIntosh & Otis, Inc.
Library of Congress Catalog Card Number: 80-23326
ISBN: 0-380-72423-5
www.avonbooks.com

First Avon Flare Printing: March 1995

Printed in the U.S.A.

10 9 8

Monday

"Owen! Time to go!"

I was spying down from behind the crest of the sand dune back of the house. Our car looked like an upside-down bug, a bug with spindly legs waving franticly in the air. Fishing rods were sticking out the back window, my bike was hanging off the rear, and the roof rack was piled with more junk than we had brought. It was the end of summer. Labor Day. Two o'clock in the afternoon. Time to go home.

But not me. I was going to stay.

"Owen! *Time to go!*"

My parents stood there, helpless, not knowing where to even begin to look for me.

"Owen!" Dad shouted again, cupping his hands around his mouth. The sound carried over the beach, over the dunes, across the East Neck. It seemed to make the marsh grass ripple, twisting the leaves slightly, green sides flashing.

"Owen!"

"He's not serious," I heard Mom say.

"Yes he is," Dad answered carefully, like he does when he's trying to make up his mind. He was dressed for the city: shoes polished, slacks creased, even a white shirt.

"His brother or sister would never have pulled a

stunt like this," my mother said. "It's absurd!" She used a hand to keep the sun's glare out of her eyes as she searched for me. "He can't stay alone."

My father checked his watch. "If he doesn't show up in five minutes, he will. Any later and *we* miss the ferry. *That's* the impossible part. We'll be stuck here."

They were really upset. That's what I had been counting on, not giving them any real choice, or time.

"I just don't believe him," Mom said wearily. "Owen!" she called again. "I bet he's out there watching and listening to us."

I was so nervous I closed my eyes.

"Where's that note of his?" my dad asked.

My mom began to read: "Dear Folks, I've decided not to go. I've decided to stay here. Don't worry. I can take care of myself. Owen."

Then my mom added: "He spelled 'decided' wrong both times."

I opened my eyes and watched my father poke the front tire with his foot. "You know how much he loves the place," he said, glancing back at the house.

"What difference does that make?" my mother burst out. "It's a dumb, immature stunt."

"But he's done it," Dad said, opening the back door of the car and pulling out my suitcase.

"What are you doing?" Mom asked, alarmed.

"We have to go, don't we? And he's determined to stay, isn't he?"

"For God's sake . . ."

"Look, he can't stay for more than a couple of days," said my father. "Let him. I'm tired of all his lecturing about how we cave in. Really, what can happen? People know him. Even the phone is working.

"Tell you what: We'll leave word in town. If Owen doesn't leave after two days, we'll have the policeman put him on the city bus. It's worth it. Two days alone, and he'll give up on his own. It's better than having him sulk for weeks." He took some bills out of his wallet. "How much do you think I should leave?"

Mom objected. "He's fourteen. He's supposed to be starting a new school."

My father looked at his watch again. "Find him. You've got two minutes."

Mom began to say something, then angrily jerked the car door open, took her seat, and slammed herself in. My suitcase in his hand, Dad hurried back to the house.

I watched him go. Having clothes and money was more than I had counted on. I only had six bucks in my pocket.

A few moments later my father was back. "Owen!" he shouted for the last time. As he got into the car I heard him say, "We'd better tell the people at Janick's that he's still here."

I lay there, heart beating wildly, not daring to move, knowing that if they saw me, they could make me leave.

"Go! Go!" I kept yelling in my head.

Car wheels spinning in the sand, they backed up, swung around, then churned up the driveway until they reached the hard road. I watched them speed away.

They were gone. And I was alone.

I lay atop the dune trying to get my breath back. It took a while. But when I did stand up, I dug my toes into the sand and looked down.

In front of me was Norton's Bay with its silent, endlessly lapping waves running seven miles west from Grenlow's Island—where I was—to the mainland at Fairport. The tide, still moving out, had left the sand glistening with seawater tears.

Off to the left was the dead-still salt marsh that marked the end of the East Neck, thick with spiky grass and firm paths of sand, a place to dig for mussels or hunt for crabs.

To the right, the long, sandy beach.

And before me, about a hundred feet above the high-water mark of twisted, dried seaweed, beyond the sea wall of wood, stood the house, the only one on the East Neck.

The house.

It's what this is all about.

More of a cabin than a house, it was supported by stilts two feet over the sand. It had been built for summer use and had only three rooms, plus a bathroom, a kitchen, and a screened-in front porch, the screens dark green from being so old. You could look out, not in.

The house had a shingle-covered roof and once white walls that had come to be a dead-fish gray. There was a chimney too, left gap-toothed by cement falling out. It didn't even stand straight. And there was an unsprung back door that, unless you shoved it tightly closed, banged out a dull tune.

Three days before Labor Day, just three days before we were supposed to leave, the girl at Janick's General Store—Terri Janick—said something to me about supposing it was my last summer in that house.

"What do you mean?" I said, startled. It was news to me.

She sort of blushed, but told me about the big hotel

complex they were about to build on the East Neck. Didn't we know?

No. No one had told us. We'd never thought to ask.

"When?" I asked.

"Soon."

The minute I got home I told my folks what was happening, that they had to do something to make sure our place wasn't touched. I mean, the Coughlin family—that's me, my father and mother, and my older brother and sister—had been coming to that house for the last three weeks in August for ten years. *Every* summer. We had to do something.

The next day this great yellow bulldozer came. Heavy, hard, its huge rusty blade at rest, it was left behind the dune back of our house.

"What's that for?" I asked the truck drivers who delivered it.

"Level the land. Knock that house down," one of the guys said, pointing to our place.

"You're kidding," I said.

"No big deal. Maybe take two minutes," he said.

I was getting sick.

I told my father he *had* to find out what was happening. Finally, the day before we were to leave, he went to see the island's real estate agent. When he came back, he avoided looking at me, just sank heavily into one of the wicker chairs.

"Well?" I said.

"It's what you found out," he told me. "They are building a hotel. Right here."

"What do you mean, *here?*"

"Here," he repeated. "Where our house is. And there's nothing we can do about it."

5

"There has to be," I said. "They don't have to do it on this spot. That's crazy."

My father shook his head. He was upset too.

"Owen," my mother urged. "Don't push."

Dad looked at me. "I'm sorry," he said. "I really am." He took the cold drink my mother offered him.

"Maybe we can find another house," Mom quickly suggested.

My father shook his head. "I spoke to the agent. Soon as word got out about the hotel, prices went high, very high. We're not coming back."

"Well," said my mother, "this isn't the only place in the world."

"It *is* the only place," I threw back.

My father shook his head. "Owen, you're talking like you were seven, not fourteen."

"Look," I said, leaning toward him. "How many places have we lived? I mean, in cities. Five, six? Come on, tell me."

"That has nothing to do with it," he said softly.

"How many," I insisted, my voice getting louder. "Seven . . . how many? You call them promotions. You know what I call them? Doing what other people tell you to do. Don't you understand? *This* is our place. We've been coming here for ten years. *Ten years!*"

"Owen," tried my mother, "we're only renters. And your father's tired. It's not as if he hasn't tried."

"He should have known," I said.

"This is supposed to be my vacation too," Dad said, trying to control his temper.

"How much were the rentals?" I demanded. "We don't have to buy."

"Owen!" my father suddenly shouted, slamming his glass to the table and slopping his drink all over.

"We are leaving tomorrow! We've had good vacation times here. We are packed. We are going. *You* are going. We are not coming back. They said we could take what we wanted, and we've cleaned the place out. The only things staying tomorrow will be the furniture and the telephone. Don't ask me why they haven't turned it off. I don't care. If anybody calls, there will be no one to answer it. Do I make myself perfectly clear? *No one!*"

I couldn't take any more. I slammed out of the house and walked down to the beach.

Right then and there—the day before we were to leave—I made up my mind. I swore to myself that I would keep that house. There was no way I was going to leave it. I just wouldn't go back to the city.

How was I going to save the place? I didn't have the slightest idea. All I knew was that I was going to do it.

And now that my parents were gone, and the first part of my plan was done, what did I feel?

Panic.

☀ A Memory of the Ninth Summer

Owen's chief memory of his ninth year on Grenlow's Island, when he was thirteen, was the first day.

Dazzling morning sun woke him. Eyes tightly shut, he let his fingers sweep the floor until he found his baseball cap, then slapped it on his head so that the peak shielded him from the light. Drawing the sheet up to his chin, he just lay there.

He had forgotten how bright the light could be on the island, so much brighter than in the city that it always took him by surprise. It didn't matter which city you lived in; daylight had nothing to do with things. In cities people woke early even in the dark. When the morning alarm sounded, the hurry began. His father off to his job, his mother to hers. Brother and sister, the same. Usually Owen was the last to leave, making sure the empty apartment had no lights left on. The Coughlins came, went, constantly busy, hardly seeing one another.

Out on the island though, for three weeks a year, nothing mattered but being easy. Loose. Together.

"Hey, Pete," Owen whispered across the room to his brother.

There was no answer.

"Hey, Pete," Owen called again. Pushing himself up on one elbow, Owen looked across to his brother's bed. It was empty. Then he remembered: In the confusion of waking Owen had forgotten that Pete, who was nineteen now, had taken a job in Vermont picking apples. He wasn't coming to the island at all this year.

Their twenty-year-old sister, Alice, wouldn't be there either. She had gone to computer school. Owen had argued with her, begged her not to go. "It won't be the same unless everybody is there," he told her.

"I need it for my job," she had explained.

Owen tried to think about what he was going to do without them. Swinging his legs out from under the sheet, he stood up and looked out the window. How quiet the mornings were, like the day before the world began.

He put on a T-shirt, shorts, and sneakers. In the bathroom he studied himself in the mirror, not liking much of what he saw.

He was big for thirteen, and as far as he was concerned, that was the only thing he had going for him.

*Older kids thought he was at least fifteen, and youn-
ger kids took him to be even older. His voice had
dropped and if he didn't talk much—no problem
there—it stayed low. His hair was curly, rarely
combed. His face was round, his eyes dark. He hid
his eyes behind tinted sunglasses. They let him look
at people without their knowing.*

*Serious-looking, he had decided it was better if he
didn't smile much, just hinted at a grin. He thought it
gave people the sense that he knew something, that
he was mysterious. He hoped so, anyway. Not that
many people knew him.*

*From the bathroom he made his way down to the
beach.*

*Deserted. That wasn't unusual. No one ever came
to the East Neck but them.*

*He began to run along the beach, keeping close to
the water's edge where the sand was firm. Once
started he pushed himself, then slowed into a pulling
stride, all but chewing on the salt-ripe air. When he
could labor no farther, he stopped running but continued to walk, heart beating fast. He was heading
for the little finger of rocks that marked the true end
of the East Neck.*

*Reaching it, he waded into the water with his
sneakers on, then climbed atop the farthest rock.
Standing there, he looked back. The house was still
visible.*

*He gazed out over the bay. A few seagulls bobbed
up and down on the soft, easy swell. The sun, more
brilliant than ever, the cloudless blue sky, were enormous.*

*Impulsively Owen shouted, "Alone!" There was no
echo, and the word, once said, vanished.*

Standing there, he began to consider what it would

be like to spend the three weeks only with his parents, without his brother and sister. Being without them seemed wrong, as if something had been forgotten.

But as he stood there, the idea came to him that he had to stop thinking that way. The important thing was that he was there, as much a part of the rock, the water, the beach, the house, as they had come to be part of him. They would always be there. Always. *He himself would hold it together. That would be his job.*

"Alone!" he shouted back at the sky. This time he threw it out loud, hard, telling himself that lasting the longest meant you won the race. To be alone meant you won.

"Alone!" he shouted again and again and again. "Alone. . . ."

The house looked empty. No bathing suits or towels hung on the back line. None of Dad's fishing junk leaned against the house. The canvas chair in which Mom liked to sit and read was gone. My rented sailboard, on which I had spent most of my time, had been returned.

It was just as strange when I went inside.

In the kitchen there were no piles of dishes in the sink, no cans of soda all over the place, no boxes of cookies, no empty ice trays.

I pulled the ceiling fixture string. At least the lights still went on.

I also checked the sink taps. Water shot out, the motor in the small pumphouse out back going on, making the water pipes rattle. It was good to hear.

I was sort of shocked not to find anything in the fridge. Nothing for sandwiches. No fruit. No pitcher of iced tea, racks of cold drinks, lemons, franks, or hamburger. Nothing.

The pantry wasn't much better. The soup cans were gone. So were the boxes of noodles and rice, the cans of tuna. All that was left was a box of moldy powdered milk and a mostly empty peanut butter jar. I used my fingers to finish that off, screwed back the top, and left the jar.

I wandered through the rest of the house. The main area, which we used as a dining, living, and play room, was just as strange. The old white wicker chairs, benches, and table made me think of skeletons. The walls, which had blue wallpaper covering, showed light blue squares where pictures of old sailing ships used to hang. Bits of straw were on the floor, the remains of the floor mats.

Still, it was in that room that I found the money Dad had left me. Ten bucks and a note:

> *Owen,*
> *Please call us tonight. We'll be expecting it.*
> *Dad*

Right off I knew *I* wasn't going to call. They would only give me arguments.

I put the money in my pocket and kept looking around. The pile of Agatha Christie mysteries my sister used to read were gone from the bottom shelf of the bookcase. Gone too were the boxes of games—checkers, Monopoly, Clue—that we always played. What was left was the Sunday paper, now a day old.

My room, the room I used to share with my brother, was just as deserted. The bed was stripped, the mattress rolled upon the iron frame and tied with a rope. Underneath were dirt balls and one tube sock. But my suitcase was in the room.

The bathroom had only a half roll of toilet paper.

My parents' room was deserted save for one of my father's slippers and the bureau with the drawers that always stuck. On top of it I found one of his butane cigarette lighters. That, at least, worked. I put it in my back pocket.

The screened-in front porch where my sister used to sleep was no livelier. All that remained was the long wooden table where we ate our meals and played matchstick poker at night or when it rained. Now it had nothing but maybe a million empty ring marks from once wet soda glasses. There was also a *Time* magazine, two weeks old.

I went out front, automatically keeping the door from slamming. My mother hated doors slamming. When I remembered she wasn't there, I went back and crashed it, loud.

For the longest time I stood on the sea wall, staring out over the bay. I could make out the mainland with the cluster of white Fairport houses. Usually the bay was full of sails, but today there were none. It was all as empty as the inside of a balloon. Everybody had gone. It felt like I was the only one left. Every once in a while I skipped a flat rock. Once I got seven jumps. But each jump was like a question: Now what? Now what? Now what?

Back came my panic.

Worse, I became scared. Sure, I'd save the house. But how? It never really had occurred to me that we wouldn't hang on somehow. I had started something, like roller skating on ice. I didn't know what to do next, or how to stop.

I made myself think of something else. Food. The nearest place to get it was Janick's, two miles away. It was something to do. I decided to put on my sneakers.

Just as I reached the porch door a voice from inside the house called out: "Hello? Is anybody home?"

It had to be the last thing I expected. More, I was sure I knew the voice, but couldn't place it.

"Anybody home?" came the call again.

Figuring I didn't have much choice, that it wouldn't matter anyway, I went into the main room.

"Yeah?" I called back, trying to make it as casual as possible.

From out of the kitchen came Terri Janick. Terri was one of the two Janick daughters, the Janicks being the island couple who ran the store where we always got gas, groceries, newspapers, stuff like that. It was usually my job to get the paper, and the person behind the newspaper counter was usually Terri. She was so much a part of the store that I think I was as surprised to see her out from behind the counter as to see her at all. Not as if we had ever talked much or anything. If she hadn't been standing right there, I don't think I could have described her.

Younger than me, she was tall and sort of thin, and she had this longish face, though her mouth was still soft and full, almost babylike. She never showed much emotion on her face, not smiling or frowning, nothing like that. She had this white stuff around her eyes, which I suppose she thought made her look cool. It didn't work. It only made her look surprised.

She was neither blond nor brown-haired, but something else. I don't know the word. The hair hung around her shoulders with sort of feathery curls. I liked the way it looked.

Considering that she lived on the island all year, I always wondered why she wasn't tan. Instead, she was more pink than anything, though she had some freckles. When I saw her that afternoon, she was dressed as she usually was—skirt, blouse, a tiny gold cross around her neck.

Truth is, I had never looked at her much before. She wasn't bad-looking. Not at all.

"Hello," she said cautiously when I came in. She was standing by the kitchen door.

"Hi," I said, keeping my voice as low as possible.

"Your folks came by on their way out," she said. "They said you were staying, and . . ." The sentence faded and her fingers wiggled nervously. "Well, you know," she said awkwardly, "they didn't say exactly, but they were, you know, unhappy about it. My mother told me to bike down and see you." She was embarrassed, like she wanted me to be sure she had no part in the idea at all.

I was annoyed anyway. "They asked your mom to check up on me?" I wanted to know.

She shrugged, tried to smile. "I guess so."

"I'm all right," I said, dropping into one of the wicker chairs and wishing she would go away. In fact, I started to flip through the newspaper.

She looked around. "You going to camp out?" she said after a while.

"No," I said, still looking at the paper.

"Aren't you supposed to go home?" she said. "It's the end of summer. You've got nothing here."

"Do *you* go home?" I asked, giving her just the right touch of half-smile.

She got red in the face. "I live here," she said softly.

"Well," I told her, "so do I." I kept turning the pages. It was the loudest sound in the room, louder even than her shifting feet.

"Since when?" she asked after a minute.

"For ten years," I said.

"Boy," she burst out, "I wouldn't stay. This island is the dullest place in the world. I'd get off so fast if I had the chance . . ." Realizing that she was talking a lot, she stopped. But then her curiosity got the best of her. "What are you going to *do?*" Her eyes suddenly got big. "You dropping out of school?"

Without thinking, I said, "I haven't made up my mind."

"What about food?" she asked.

"I've got money."

She didn't question that either. In fact, she didn't say anything, just stood there.

I decided I had to do something. I got up, standing as tall as I could. "I was just going over to your store to get some stuff."

I went into my room and put on my sneakers. When I came out, she was gone. That was fine with me. But when I went outside, she was standing by her bike, waiting.

"I was just supposed to find out how you were," she said, almost like an apology. "My school starts Wednesday," she added. "I've still got to go." She made a face that I suppose was meant to say she didn't really want to. Then she started to push her bike along the driveway. But at the end she stopped and looked back. She had caught sight of the bulldozer.

"You do know about your house, don't you?" she said.

"Yeah," I said, standing there, hands in back pockets. "You told me."

"It's supposed to happen soon."

"That's the whole point," I told her. "I don't intend to let them."

That took her by surprise. "You don't?" she said. "Nope."

She looked at me for a moment. It was a different kind of look than before. "You going to tell that to Miss Devlin?"

"Who's she?" I asked, never having heard the name before.

"She owns the place," said Terri. "She owns most of the island. She lets Mr. Marcus, the real estate agent, handle things, but it's really her."

I suppose I should have known that, but I wasn't going to admit it. So I just said, "Oh, yeah, her."

For a moment Terri stood there, then she turned away. "Well," she said, "see you." She got on her bike and moved off.

I watched her go, then asked myself why I hadn't been nicer. I could even have gone with her to the store. But then I'm not very good with people. By the time I thought about changing my mind, she had gone too far. I watched as she went down the beach road, then I turned around and stared into the marsh.

☀ A Memory of the Third Summer

It was five in the afternoon. Seven-year old Owen was tired of building sand castles. His mother was in the kitchen, making supper. His father had not come back yet from fishing. His brother, Pete, was lying on the beach, working on his suntan.

"Pete?" said Owen.

"Yeah."

"Want to go into the marsh and catch fiddler crabs?"

"Nope."

16

"You said you would."

"Tomorrow," suggested Pete.

"I want to go now."

"I'm too lazy," said Pete.

Owen next approached his sister, Alice, who was propped up against a folding backrest, reading a mystery. She was always reading mysteries.

"Alice," said Owen, "I'm going to look for fiddler crabs. Want to come?"

Alice looked up and smiled. "You really love those little buggers, don't you?"

"They're funny," said Owen. "They run all over the place. Like crazy."

"Don't you worry they'll nip you?" she said, giving her little brother a playful pinch.

"Naw," said Owen. "They just tickle. Want to come?"

"I've got to finish this book. I'm almost at the end. It's the best part. How about later?"

"Nope. Too late."

"Go by yourself, then," Alice suggested. She smiled at him warmly. "Bring back some for me."

"O.K.," said Owen. He ran to get his plastic pail and shovel, then poked his head into the kitchen to shout, "Mom, I'm going to get some fiddler crabs!"

"Don't be too long," she called back. "Dinner's almost ready."

It had been a hot day. Now it was rapidly cooling off. A slight breeze had come. The tide was low. There were some clouds. For a moment Owen felt chilled. But gripping both pail and shovel he bravely entered the marsh, taking one of the sandy pathways they had trampled down on the way to the soft-shelled clam bed.

The grass was high for Owen, but not so high that

he couldn't see over it. He marched forward. Once he did look back and was able to see the house. He felt sure he knew where he was.

Farther along the pathway he found an old conch shell, bleached white. He bent down to examine it, studying it from different angles, then decided to bring it home. Placing it in his pail, he stood up. Only then did he realize that he had forgotten which way he had been going, which way he had come.

He looked for the house. He couldn't find it. There was nothing to see but grass.

Puzzled, he continued on, stepping through the grass. He didn't go very far before he realized he was lost.

"Mom!" he shouted. There was no answer. "Dad!"

No sound came back. Still, knowing he could not be too lost, he stood there, sucking on his lower lip, biting it, trying to think which way to go.

Feeling the need to move, he rushed forward, un-expectedly coming upon a little lagoon, a pool of still, black seawater. The moment he broke through the grass hundreds of fiddler crabs, each no more than an inch wide, danced away.

Owen laughed, forgetting his fears. He squatted down and watched.

He stayed that way for a long time, carefully study-ing the crabs. But when he looked up he was startled to see that a bird had come to the middle of the pool. Large and white, pure white, it was standing on one tall foot. Its long beak, almost red, glistened. A tiny black eye seemed to glow. From time to time it bent its slender neck into the pool and poked about.

Never in his life had Owen seen anything so beau-tiful.

He stood up, excited. The bird, seeming not to notice, went on with its slow, careful feeding.

"Bird," whispered Owen.

The bird, unafraid, lifted its head and looked at Owen. Its black eye, rimmed by yellow, blinked.

Owen reached out toward it with both hands. He wanted to touch it, to capture it, to bring it home and keep it forever. But something startled the bird, for as Owen reached, it spread its enormous white wings and leaped into the air.

"Bird!" cried Owen. "Come back!"

The bird flew away. That time Owen did cry, and he was still crying when Pete burst through the grass.

"There you are, crazy. Hey, don't cry. You're not lost anymore."

"I was watching the bird," said Owen, wiping his tears away as he hugged his big brother. "But it flew away. Is it going to come back?"

"Sure," said Pete soothingly. "Birds always come back if you wait long enough. But dinner's ready. Hot franks. Grab your pail." And taking Owen by the hand, he led his little brother home.

All the way, Owen kept looking back over his shoulder, hoping the bird would return, promising himself that he would stay until it did.

I felt a little foolish about not going with Terri, so I decided not to go to Janick's for food right away. Instead, I had a swim, after which I lay down on the beach, really tired. If I had had some paper I would have written to my brother and sister. I wanted to tell them what I was doing. They didn't come to the island anymore, but I was sure they would have understood.

But there was no paper. All I could do was think

out what I might have said. Not that I got far. I fell asleep. So it wasn't till around five o'clock in the afternoon that I set out for food, money in my pocket.

Janick's General Store was a little more than two miles away. But then, nothing was ever far away on the island. It's only seventeen square miles in size.

I always liked to walk to the store. In my head, whenever I needed to measure a mile or two, I used that walk. It was my ruler for the rest of the world.

The first mile was along the beach where at any point you could stop, turn, and see where the house stood. Then, making a sharp bend, the road led inland, out of the East Neck. Quickly, green foliage blocked out the smells and sounds of the bay. What came next was this ripe, heavy sense of late summer, a rotting and growing all at once.

The few houses you passed were all set deep back behind driveways, so you couldn't tell much about the people who lived there. You couldn't even tell if they were about. Beyond that came farms where a few of the locals lived and worked.

On the whole island the year-round population was hardly seven hundred, though during the summer it went up to three times that. To get onto the island you had to use a ferry that ran six times a day. Kids left the island regularly because the junior and senior high schools were on the mainland. I guess the adults just stayed and stayed.

It was funny: Prices were high, but people on the island were kind of poor. There was some fishing and farming, but most of the money the locals made came from summer people.

All these facts about the island weren't anything I knew firsthand. When I was on the island, I kept pretty much to the East Neck. But I had heard my folks talk.

The town center was small, six white buildings all in a row: a town hall, the volunteer fire department garage, an old store that some summer people had made into an art gallery, Mort's Fish and Tackle Shop, a clothing store, and at the end of the row, Janick's General Store.

Janick's Store—All You'll Ever Need, said the sign over the door in fake old-fashioned letters. It was pretty true. You could buy aspirin, greeting cards, a hamburger, a Ping-Pong ball. It was a gas station, grocery store, luncheonette, post office, and odds-and-ends sort of place all in one. Each member of the Janick family ran a section. I used to wonder if they had five departments so that everybody could have something to do or if there were five of them so that they could do the work.

I took my time reaching the store. When I got close, I saw Bill Janick, the Janicks' eighteen-year-old son, washing down one of the gas pumps with a bucket of soapy water.

He had blond hair and wore it long. He was strong—or he looked strong—and he had a dark tan. I think I wanted to look like him. Like Terri, his face was kind of sharp. But unlike her, he was jumpy and on edge most of the time. He was always moving around.

Bill wasn't much of a friend or anything but I had known him for a long time. So I called out, "Hi!"

He didn't say a word. He just looked up and frowned. It caught me by surprise. That wasn't the way islanders usually treated me.

When I got inside the store, I had another surprise. The day before it had been crowded. People had been lined up getting their Sunday papers from Terri. Others had been at the soda counter, drinking coffee, eating doughnuts, being served by the eldest Janick daughter, Pam, whom I really liked to look at. And in the post office corner, Mrs. Janick was talking to some people. Mr. Janick, behind his grocery counter, had been listening to a political conversation.

But now the store was deserted. The wooden floor, the brass fixtures, the big wall clock, the luncheonette counter—they all seemed dark, quiet, asleep. The only brightness was a yellow funnel of sunlight that flowed through the door window, changing the swirling dust into golden flecks.

I looked about, half hoping to see Terri. She wasn't there. I was just about to go out and ask Bill for the things I wanted when I noticed the top of Mr. Janick's head behind the grocery counter.

Mr. Janick had always seemed old to me. He had a mane of white hair and was very short, and the eyeglasses he wore must have been at least an inch thick. He got about on crutches, and slowly at that. Something about a car accident. But he used those crutches to tip stuff down from top shelves. When I was a kid, that had fascinated me. He always made me think of an old, wounded lion.

I walked up to the counter, about to speak to him, when I realized he was asleep. His head kept dropping down, jerking back, dropping again.

Hoping he would wake up, I looked over the shelves. There wasn't much left. I finally decided on some spaghetti, two cans of tuna, a carton of milk, cold cereal, bread, and peanut butter.

When Mr. Janick kept on sleeping, I wasn't sure what to do. Finally I picked up a jar of jam displayed on the counter and rapped it down. His head snapped up instantly, and his eyes, distant behind the glasses he wore, opened up on me.

For a moment he didn't know who I was. Then he remembered. "The Coughlin boy," he said, struggling to come to his feet with the help of crutches. He examined me as if he were reading a label. "Your parents said call." He spoke in short sentences that might have been torn from a first-grade reader. He had a trace of a foreign accent.

"I will," I said, annoyed that everybody seemed to know what I was doing.

"What do you want?" he asked. Usually he smiled. This time, nothing.

When I told him, he struggled up and down the aisle, fetching things, while I kept thinking how much faster it would have been if I did it for myself.

After he got the stuff, he wrote out the cost of everything on a bag, tapping down the column with a pencil. Finally he announced the total: "Six fifty-two."

"Six fifty-two?" I said. I hadn't expected it to be that much.

"It's correct," he said stiffly.

I paid, but just before he handed me my change, he said, "You told Terri you don't wish the hotel. That's why you're staying. You're making trouble."

"Sorry," I mumbled, picking up my bag, and not liking to talk about it to him.

"Why?" he demanded.

Not wanting to get into a discussion, I said nothing.

"It's none of your business," he said. "You musn't make problems."

I just looked at him, wishing people would be more friendly and less nosy, then went out the door.

23

When I came out, Bill Janick was there. Four other guys, friends of his, were there too. They had been talking and laughing loudly. The minute they saw me, they shut up and looked me over.

Right away I got nervous. Something was really wrong. Still, I got out a "Hello." Then, since they didn't give me any choice, I had to walk right through them. And, moving away, I was sure they were staring after me.

Swearing under my breath, I didn't dare look around to let them sense that I was scared. I just kept going, moving faster than I normally did, hoping it didn't look that way. I didn't think they would bother me—but I wasn't sure.

I took a nervous look over my shoulder, trying to make it seem as if I were checking out a tree. They were there all right, still watching.

I didn't want to, but I quickened my pace, taking longer strides, making my eyes keep straight down the road. I was working so hard at it that I actually jumped when a clanging noise burst right behind me. I spun about, expecting to be slammed. It was Terri on her bike.

She must have realized that she had scared me because she got confused and could hardly get out what she wanted to say.

"My mother says would you like to have dinner with us?" she said.

It was the last thing I expected. I didn't know how to answer. I almost wanted to, but when I looked past her, I saw that her brother and his friends were still watching.

"No," I said. "Maybe another time. I've got my dinner here."

Then I marched off, not saying another thing, leaving her in the middle of the road.

I was halfway home before I remembered that there wasn't a cooking pot in the house.

✳ A Memory of the Eighth Summer

Though it was a hot afternoon Owen and his father walked to Janick's. Owen had his new baseball mitt with him, a present for his twelfth birthday. All the way there, he kept throwing the ball high in the air and catching it in the new mitt.

"Keep your eyes on the road," his father cautioned. "There are cars, you know."

But not one car passed.

They were both hot when they reached the store, and Mr. Coughlin suggested that Owen have a soda while he chatted with Mr. Janick.

Owen climbed onto the luncheonette stool, which looked so much like a mushroom. Bill Janick was behind the counter.

"I want a Coke," Owen announced.

Bill carefully finished wiping down the counter, then got the drink ready.

While he waited to be served, Owen kept pounding the glove with the ball, trying to work in a pocket. But when the soda came, Owen rested the glove on the counter. Bill Janick looked at it.

"Nice glove you've got there," he said to Owen.

"It's new," said Owen proudly. "I got it for my birthday. It's got Carl Yastrzemski's name on it."

"Hey, nice," said Bill. "Can I take a look?"

"Sure," said Owen, sucking on the straw.

Bill picked up the glove carefully and examined the stitching. "Nice," he repeated. "You a Boston fan?"

"Sure," said Owen. "We lived there once."

"Get to see them play?" asked Bill.

"We didn't have time."

"Collect baseball cards?"

"Got a whole box. Wish I had a Yaz card. I don't, though. They're hard to get."

Bill had put the glove on and was slapping his hand into it. "Hey," he said. "How about a catch?"

"Yeah," said Owen. Without finishing his drink, he swiveled down and raced for the door.

Once outside, Owen was a bit puzzled about what to do. Bill still had his glove, and Owen was too shy to ask for it back.

"Want to pitch some?" suggested Bill. "I bet you've got a good arm."

Flattered, Owen went beyond the gas pump, out on the road. Bill, glove still on his hand, crouched low.

"One finger means fast ball, two is a curve, three is a slow change up," he shouted, instantly giving a one-finger sign.

Owen looked down at Bill, nodded seriously, took a full windup, then flung the ball. Bill had to leap high to pull it down.

"Hey, with a glove like this, you gotta do better than that," he said, crouching again. "Chuck it in, baby, chuck it in. Don't make me work." He put down two fingers.

Owen, not knowing how to throw a curve, shook him off.

Bill gave the same sign.

Owen, decided he had no choice, wound up and threw the ball in, this time good enough to make him feel better. Bill had to move only a little.

"Attaboy! Attaboy! Way to go! Way to go!" cried Bill. "See if you can throw it straight. A pro glove means a pro arm. Let's see if you deserve it."

After rolling the ball back to Owen, Bill gave the slow-ball sign.

Owen threw the ball wild. High over Bill's head it sailed, landing way down the road. Disgusted, Bill stood with his hands on hips, looking after it. Owen, not sure what to do, waited for Bill to get it.

Suddenly Bill turned on him. "What you waiting for?" he snapped.

"The ball," said Owen.

"Look, kid," said Bill. "I'm not behind the counter now. Fetch your own stuff."

Slowly, Owen walked to where the ball lay. When he returned, Bill had gone. The glove lay in the middle of the road.

Owen's father was just coming out of the store. "I wouldn't leave your glove in the road like that," he cautioned. "A car might crush it."

Owen quickly picked up the glove. To his relief, nothing was wrong with it.

"What's the matter?" his father asked. "You and Bill have an argument?"

Owen, not saying anything, looked around for some sign of the older boy. Bill was nowhere to be seen. But all the way home Owen kept trying to understand why Bill had been angry with him.

It was dusk when I reached the house. For a moment I just stood in the middle of the kitchen, uncomfortable with the house and its empty feeling. Usually it felt crowded, almost as if a party were going on all the time.

I suppose I knew I could have gone back and exchanged the food I couldn't use, but I didn't want to make a fool of myself. More to the point, I didn't want to see Bill Janick and his friends. I was beginning to get a sense of what their stares and silences were all about, and it was making me worried. They didn't like what I was doing. That was clear enough. As far as I was concerned, that was just tough. It wasn't any of their business. But that didn't help me feel better.

I put the bag of groceries on the sink counter, took out what I had bought, and decided to eat the tuna. Then I remembered that there was no can opener either. All I could find to eat with in the kitchen were some pieces of plastic picnic stuff—a fork, some spoons, and a knife. That, some nails, and a special tool that the propane gas man had once left was all there was.

I opened the peanut butter. Stabbing the plastic knife into the jar, I tried to scoop out a gob, only to have the plastic snap.

So did my temper. I flung the knife handle across the room, then dug my fingers into the peanut butter and spread it on the bread.

I made three sandwiches, went to the main room, dumped the *Time* magazine, sat on the rocking chair, and ate as if I were just waiting for *them* to do something about the house right then and there. Waiting for the bulldozer.

"Stupid," I said out loud, getting that panicky feeling again. Sitting there, rocking, I began to tell myself that I had to plan something, *anything*. I had done the first thing—stay. The question was, what next? I couldn't just wait.

I grabbed my last sandwich and went outside to look over the bay. It had gotten darker, but I could make out the beach line and hear the lapping of the waves. Out to the west there was a crimson line, the last edge of the day, like the crack in a doorway just before it's closed. I asked myself if I was inside or out. Even as I watched, that last edge snapped up tight and dark. The door was locked, and I wondered what would happen.

I was just standing there when I heard the phone ring. It made me jump. I hurried back to the kitchen and grabbed the phone.

" 'Lo?" I said.

"Owen?"

My father's voice. A minute before, it might have been great to talk to someone. The second I heard his voice I didn't want to talk at all.

"Yeah," I said. "This is Owen."

"This is your dad."

"I know. What's up?" I said, realizing right away that wasn't the best thing to say.

"What's up with *you?* should be the question."

"I'm O.K."

"Frankly, Owen, I don't know what to say," my father said carefully. "To be perfectly honest I think you've done a rather—unwise thing."

"Well," I said. "I don't agree."

"Look, we were all fond of the house," he said. "I promise you, we'll make every effort to find something for next summer. How about it?"

"No."

"How long do you intend to stay?" my father tried, and I could sense that he was trying to keep from losing his temper. "One or two days is no big deal, but—how long, Owen?"

"I don't know. Long as I need to."

There was this pause. I could hear his breathing, each breath like another layer of patience peeling off. "There's no way to save it," he said at last.

"Maybe," I said. "Maybe not."

"Owen, my experience—" His voice started to go up with his temper, but he caught it.

"Here's your mother," he said quickly. "She wants to speak to you." Then he must have put his hand over the phone because I heard only muffled voices at the other end.

"Owen?" It was my mother.

"Yes, Mom," I said, already sick of being hassled.

"I don't know what to say," she started off. "Are you all right? Do you have enough food? Did the Janicks get in touch with you as I asked them to?"

"Mom, I've got lots of food, I'm getting plenty of sleep, and I brush my teeth after every bite."

"Owen, I—"

"Mom," I cut in, exasperated. "I don't want to argue with you. I know what I'm doing."

Then she said, "What *are* you doing?" She was really asking a question.

Her not understanding made me angrier than ever. "You know what it is!" I shouted, and slammed down the phone.

I stood there, one hand balled up into a fist. Right away, the phone started to ring again. It was like they were screaming at me. I shot out my hands, grabbed the cord that connected the phone to the wall, and yanked it out.

The ringing stopped. I picked up the phone and listened. The line was dead.

Exhausted, I went around looking for the peanut butter sandwich I was sure I hadn't eaten. Not finding it in the house, I went out to the front porch. I didn't find it there either. But through the screen I saw the headlights of a car bearing down along the beach road a half mile away.

The beach road was a dead end. There was no place to come but to our place.

As the car drew closer, I became more and more edgy. When it stopped at the end of our driveway, the motor died and the lights went out. My first thought was that it was Bill Janick and his buddies, the ones that had given me the bad looks at the store.

Afraid of what they might do, I stood perfectly still, then made up my mind to get out of there. I went out through the porch, making sure not to let the door slam.

As quietly as I could, I moved out to the far side of the house, stopping at the corner where it was darkest. Then I listened.

At first I couldn't hear anything. Then I heard a laugh coming from the car. I could also hear murmuring voices, but couldn't make out what they were saying.

I clung to the dark corner, ready to run, telling myself there was no way I would mix with them.

When a car door opened, I braced myself. Then someone shouted, "Time to go home!" The next thing I heard was a splintering crash on the roof right over my head. Glass bits of a broken bottle spattered, then showered down all around me.

The car door slammed, the lights and motor burst on, and the car, grinding gravel, made a shrieking U-turn and sped away. All I could see were the trailing red lights.

I was trembling.

Even so, I was awfully glad that they—whoever

they were—had gone. I wondered if they had been trying to hit me with the bottle or had aimed for the house. Whichever it was, one thing was clear: The message was, "Go!"

Still trembling, I went back into the house and turned off all the lights except those in my own room and took my radio from my suitcase.

I plugged in the radio and found a station that played music I liked, but kept it quieter than normal. Then I unrolled my mattress and lay down, feet hanging over the end of the bed, and just stared up at the ceiling.

It took a while before I calmed down. By that time, I was trying to make up my mind whether I should stay or go.

I mean, I was scared.

I knew perfectly well that I could go back to the city and tell my parents that I had decided to listen to them. They would have been so glad they wouldn't ask questions. They wouldn't have to know what happened.

But *I* would.

It wasn't anything about being a coward. That wasn't it at all. The point was, I had made myself a promise to save the house. That was the hard part. The only way I could save it was by staying. No other way. None.

Thinking so hard gave me a headache. I tried to listen to music, even made the radio louder. But it didn't work. I kept having the same thought: How was I going to save the house?

Then the news came on. It was all about what was doing all over the world, all that stuff, and about how many people were going to get themselves killed on the road over the Labor Day weekend.

And I said to myself, "The road isn't the only place you can get killed."

Somewhere in the middle of the newscast I fell asleep, but my God, I knew that saving the house was going to be hard. And I hadn't guessed the half of it.

Tuesday

When I awoke the next morning, I felt stiff and dirty from sleeping in my clothes. Worse, I had no idea what time it was. All I knew was that the house was full of bright, white light and the radio had nothing but static. I turned it off.

For a long time I lay on the bed, sorting out my thoughts, trying to think what to do next, reminding myself that I had made the decision to stay. Though the sunlight made me feel better, I kept thinking about the way people were reacting: Bill, Mr. Janick, Terri, the bottle throwers. Just thinking about it brought back uneasy feelings.

What got me up was the notion of going swimming.

The tide was still high as I went down to the beach. I looked up and down the water's edge and out into the bay, reminding myself that I could get some clams or mussels when the tide went down. I could always eat the clams raw.

Breaking into a run, I plunged into the water, the only way to beat the cold. It hits you like a shot, then it's gone.

The moment I was underwater I felt better. I swam deep and touched the bottom, opening my eyes against the murk. I loved it. It's a fantasy world. I could explore it forever. Hey, Aquaman!

Later, while I ate a breakfast of peanut butter sandwiches and milk, I decided on my next step. Terri Janick had mentioned the woman—I had already forgotten her name—who owned the island. The more I thought about it, the more the idea that I might be able to find her and convince her not to rip the house down appealed to me. It was such a simple idea that the possibility of trying it, making her listen to reason, had me congratulating myself. From the way Terri had spoken, no one had even tried. I would.

Anyway, just having a plan of action made me feel better.

In fact, it made me feel so much better that when I finished eating, I thought about the spaghetti and tuna problem again and made up my mind to exchange what I couldn't use. I didn't care what the Janicks thought. Besides, I figured I wouldn't meet up with Bill Janick or his friends so early in the morning.

So I got into dry clothes, put on my sunglasses, and started off.

The only trouble was that when I reached Janick's store, I found the *Closed* sign posted outside the door. I put my face to the glass door and looked in at the wall clock. It was after seven. I must have gotten up about five. No wonder the radio only gave static. They hadn't even started broadcasting! I don't think I have ever gotten up so early on my own in my life.

Feeling more idiotic than ever, I thought of going home and returning later. At the same time I tried to recall what time the store usually opened. When I realized opening time couldn't be much later than eight or eight-thirty, I decided to wait it out and think out what I was trying to do.

✳ A Memory of the Sixth Summer

It had started out in the most ordinary fashion with Owen, who was ten that summer, deciding to build a sand castle, as he had done thousands of times before.

The tide, though rising, was still low, the best time to build. As the water came back, you could make moats and they would fill.

Owen didn't make sand castles in the usual way. He had his own methods. First he got a coffee can and punched a few nail holes in the bottom, small holes and not too many. He filled the can with soupy wet sand, then let the water drain. What remained was moist but very firm. A quick flip of the can, and he had a perfect tower. By using different-size cans, he could make all kinds of towers, some on top of one another.

Even that wasn't the special thing.

When a few towers were up, Owen gathered a handful of ready wet sand and with great care let it drip out between his fingers. The effect was magical; the sand, trickling down in a small stream, built into fantastic shapes, strange shapes, light and airy shapes, lace of sand. He could make the towers tall, sharp as needles, and if he was super careful, into archways and bridges, castle to castle.

It was magical.

That afternoon was special. He hadn't meant the castles to be any different from those he had done before. But that day, he never knew why, everything had worked perfectly. Castle after castle went up. He kept thinking they all might topple, collapse, or just melt away. It didn't happen. They became more than castles. They became a city—a world.

"Hey, Mom, look what Owen's doing," Alice cried.

Mrs. Coughlin came and looked. By then the city was about three feet square and still growing.

"I wish Boston looked like that," his mother said. They would be moving to Boston right after Labor Day.

Owen looked up at her, not certain what she meant.

"Don't get sunburned, Owen," she said. "Put on a shirt."

Owen kept working, and his sister stayed on to watch.

"Want some help?" she offered.

"No, thanks. I can do it."

"It really is nice," she told him.

"Thanks," he said, and kept working.

When his brother and father came back from fishing, the castle city was three times as big and getting more and more glorious each moment. There were close to a hundred towers, linked, tunneled, threaded by moats.

"Hey, man, that's neat," said Pete. "Dad," he called to his father, "you see what Owen did?"

His father finished hauling up the rowboat, then came to look, silently studying the sand-castle city.

Owen glanced up at him.

"That's pretty big," said his father. "Lot of work."

"Yeah," said Owen, not stopping.

"You do know the tide's coming in."

"I know."

"I just didn't want you to be surprised."

"Catch anything?" asked Owen.

"Few porgies and a bass," said Pete, and he and his father went to clean them.

Owen stayed with his castles. The water, rising higher, slid into the moats. In some places towers began to cave in. In other spots erosion made it all the more interesting.

Owen kept working.

The tide attacked the city. In response Owen worked faster, trying to build the city away from the water.

A sudden wave curled in, washing away a wall of defense.

As if the water were fire, Owen jumped back and looked down at the damage. Not much. The city was still almost ten feet wide, five feet deep.

"Owen!" he heard his mother call. "Dinner time!"

"Be there in a second," he shouted back. But he stayed, trying to build a defense. He knew then that he was working to save the city, trying to build a deeper moat that would allow the water to run around it, to make an island against the attack.

But the moat didn't work. Water continued to flood in and soon began to demolish the city from the rear.

Realizing that the moat had been a mistake, Owen frantically filled it in.

"Owen!" his father shouted from the house. "Dinner's on the table!"

"Coming!"

He stayed though, watching as tower after tower melted beneath the rising tide.

"Dinner, Owen," yelled his brother. "We're all waiting. Mom says if you don't come now, you'll have to eat alone."

Desperate, Owen didn't know what to do. If he left,

39

there would be no chance at all of saying his city. If he stayed, he just might.

"Owen!" shouted his father angrily. "Stop this foolishness. Come this instant!"

With a last look back, Owen went into the house.

Only when dinner and chores were done was Owen allowed to come out again. By then his magical city had been badly torn and broken. Only a few tall towers poked above the shallow water.

And by next morning, when Owen went down to the water's edge, the sand where he had built his city was as smooth and flat as everywhere else on the beach. It was as if his city had never existed. Ever.

After that Owen didn't build any more sand castles. Ever.

I had been waiting about forty-five minutes in front of Janick's store when a huge gasoline delivery truck pulled up and stopped in front of where I was sitting.

"Morning," the driver called down.

"Morning," I said.

"Janick's not open yet?"

"Opens at eight," I said, hoping I was right.

"Sleepy times are here again!" the driver sang out as he climbed down. He opened the ground storage tank cap, lowered his measuring rod, pulled it up, and whistled. "Guess those summer folk took it all and ran. Almost empty."

I could tell he thought I was a local.

After hooking up his hose to the tank, he set the gas pumping, then sat down next to me. "Smoke?" he offered, drawing out a cigarette pack from his pocket.

"No thanks," I said, though I felt like telling him

he was crazy, that he might blow us both up. A gas man once told me stories about explosions.

"You're smart, kid," he said, lighting up and inhaling deeply. "When I was your age, I'd been smoking for years. No good."

Nervously I watched him wave the burned-out match, relaxing only when he put it in his pocket.

"Guess you're glad to have the island to yourself again, eh?" he said. "Good to have the summer people go. Over to Fairport, where I live, it's the same. They look down on you. Demanding this, demanding that. And they don't live here. What do you do for them? Mow lawns or something? Picking up after them. Well, you figure, long as they got the money you have to do what they want. Right? Money pays the winter bills. And it's only two months they're here. Then off they go, and you're nobody's slave. Oh, I know."

A bell jangled. We both looked up. It was Terri opening the door.

"Hi there, lass," the driver called out. "Got your gas there, pumping."

"Thanks," she said. After turning the *Closed* sign around to read *Open*, she went back inside.

Feeling a little uneasy, I followed her inside, waiting as she went and put the lights on. Only when she got behind the food counter did she say "Hi" to me.

I took the things out of the bag. "I bought these yesterday," I explained. "But when I got home I remembered I didn't have a cooking pot. Or," I added, feeling like a complete jackass, "a can opener."

She didn't say anything, just looked at me.

"Can I return them?" I asked.

She frowned, but after looking around to see if anybody was watching, she said, "You're not supposed to, but I guess you can." She pulled my things out of the bag. "What do you want instead?"

I hadn't even considered that.

"You could buy a can opener," she said.

"Yeah, right," I said as quickly as I could. "I was going to ask you about that. You have one?"

She hurried across the store to her regular area. From beneath the glass-covered counter with the nail clippers, Ping-Pong balls, playing cards, and other odd bits she lifted an opener. "Now what?" she said when she put it down before me.

"Maybe I'll keep the tuna," I said. "What about some packages of soup? I could cook them in the tuna cans."

"Is your stove working?" she said.

"I guess so," I answered, feeling like a baby for not having checked. "The propane tank is still there."

"What kind of soup do you want?" she said.

I studied the shelves. "Mushroom. I'll take mushroom."

She fetched four packages and as her father had done, wrote out the prices on a bag. "Two dollars."

I paid her, took up the bag, and headed out, stopping at the door as if I had just remembered. "Oh," I said, "you mentioned something yesterday about that lady who owns the land, you know. . . ."

"Miss Devlin?"

"That's the one. She live on the island?"

"She has a home out at the Point."

"She here? I mean, on the island now?"

"I don't know. Why?"

"I thought I'd go speak to her, try to convince her not to bust up the house."

"Speak to her?" said Terri, making it sound as if it were the most impossible thing she had ever heard.

"Why not? Something the matter with that?"

Terri shook her head. "I don't think anyone talks to her. She does the talking."

I put on my best half-smile. "I will," I let Terri know. "Thanks for the exchange," I said, and started for the door.

Just as I reached it, I looked out through the glass and saw the town's one police car parked outside. Standing talking to the truck driver was the policeman, Mr. Bermoldi. I froze.

"What is it?" asked Terri, who had seen my reaction.

"It's the cop."

"Ed? Is he looking for you?"

I quickly backed away from the door. "I don't know. My parents said they were going to get him to send me home." I searched around to see if there was another way out.

Terri was looking at me as if she couldn't believe what I was doing.

"Look," I told her. "Last night some people smashed a bottle on my house, told me to get out. You're the only one acting decent around here."

"Ed won't hurt you," she whispered. "He's not from the island. Doesn't feel the same way."

"Yeah? That gas man out there isn't from the island either. Ask him what he thinks of summer people. You have a back way out?"

She came slowly from behind the counter, then, making up her mind, quickly led me through a kind of pantry storeroom. At the far end was a door.

"Cut across the town hall," she told me as she opened the door. "He won't see you."

Bag of soup and tuna in one hand, I took the wooden steps in a jump, turned, and looked up at her.

"Thanks," I told her, really feeling it. "I appreciate it." Then I began to run as fast as I could.

I reached the house famished. Once there, I used my new can opener and attacked the tuna with a plastic fork, gobbling it all down right from the can. Considering that tuna tastes awful that way, it wasn't bad. In fact, I ate the second can too.

I topped that off with a peanut butter sandwich that I ate sitting on the front steps, watching the bay and trying to work out how I'd approach Miss Devlin.

First I tried a whole set speech, but gave that up fast, deciding just to go and hope she'd be reasonable.

As far as I was concerned, I was dressed perfectly fine, but I knew my parents wouldn't think so. And if they didn't, I assumed that this Miss Devlin, who was probably like them or older, wouldn't think too much of me either.

From my suitcase I got out an Adidas T-shirt I'd been saving for school. I also pulled out the pair of white jeans I had recently bought—in a sort of deal I had made with Mom when she wanted me to get some dress-up stuff.

I slicked down my hair with water, tied my running shoes with double knots, got my sunglasses in place, and checked myself out in the mirror. The only problem was on my nose: a small zit.

Backing off, I looked again at myself. Except for the fact that my ears are too big—and my hair hides that—I didn't look too bad. Not great, but not bad.

I practiced my half-smile. I have it down pat: a slight squint to the eyes, head cocked slightly to one side, just one corner of my mouth up. If I get it too low, it's a smirk. Too high, and it looks like I've had a stroke. I figure if I could lift one eyebrow, I could have it really perfect.

I tried working the one eyebrow, but all that happened was a general widening of both eyes, which I had to admit made me look like a fish of small brain. So, using one finger, I moved my right eyebrow up and down fifteen minutes, supposing that exercising the right muscles couldn't hurt.

A quick brush to the old teeth, deodorant, and I was ready.

The Point, where Miss Devlin lived, was clear across the other side of the island, by road about five miles. It was the ritzy part of the island, with huge houses, big lawns, gardens carefully hidden behind pine trees and curvy driveways. Show me a curvy driveway, and I'll show you money.

I don't think there were more than twenty of those mansions there. The people who owned them thought of themselves as a separate community. They even had their own fancy dock with a gas pump and a shower house.

The entrance to the Point—brick squares on either side of the road—made you know it was exclusive. One square had a wooden sign: *The Point Community.* The other square had its sign: *Private Road. No Trespassing.*

I went in anyway.

Once inside, I had no idea where this Miss Devlin might be. None of the houses had names on them. I guess you were just supposed to know. Worse, all the houses looked the same: great white columns holding up huge roofs, like the set for *Gone With the Wind.* The place didn't seem to have people. When I finally did see someone, it was a man on a ladder repainting a fence.

"Morning," he said politely when I went up to him.

"I'm looking for Miss Devlin's house," I said.

Right away he became suspicious. "What do you want her for?"

"I need to talk to her."

"What about?"

"Private business," I said, not believing how everywhere I went people wanted to know what I was doing.

"I'm not so sure she's about," he said. "It was Labor Day yesterday. Most folks hereabouts go home."

"Well, I didn't and I still need to talk to her. She here?"

He studied me carefully. "Her house is the last one," he said after a while. "Right on the Point." He showed the way with a hand.

"Thanks," I said, starting off, even though I knew he was watching me.

The closer I came to the end of the road, the more nervous I got. Then I saw the house, and right away I understood what the other houses were to this one. Miss Devlin's house wasn't just the oldest. It was the biggest. A real mansion. The others on the Point just imitated hers. Hers looked right, real and rich.

There was no hedge, only a tall iron fence, the gate half open. Inside was a fancy blue European car. Someone was home.

I stood before the door, trying to imagine what she would look like, still hoping to get some idea how to speak. It was useless. In the end I had to force myself to push the door button, half hoping that no one would be there. From deep inside I heard a chime. But no one came.

I pushed the button again and waited. When still

46

no one came, I turned around in time to see the man who had given me directions watching me from the road.

Even as I was giving him a dirty look, the door behind me opened.

A young woman stood there. Her long, dark hair was a mess and hung about her face. Her shirt—a man's shirt—was just as much a muck. Not only was it too big for her but it was spattered with paint. So were the jeans she wore, and her hands and bare feet.

"Yes?" she said to me.

"Oh, hi," I said, relieved that at least I wouldn't have to deal with Miss Devlin right off. "I'm looking for Miss Devlin," I said.

"What can I do for you?" she said. "I'm Miss Devlin."

Miss Devlin might have been anyone, anyone that is except a good-looking young woman. I didn't have much of a set speech, but when I saw that it was her standing right in front of me, whatever I had blew away. Worse, I could see she wasn't exactly happy about coming to the door. She pushed the hair out of her eyes, only managing to add an extra streak of paint to her forehead. I must have arrived right in the middle of her painting something. It was clear she wanted to get back to it.

"My name is Owen Coughlin," I said. "I live . . . my folks and I . . . we're from the city and we've been renting the place along Norton's Bay. The East Neck place. For ten years."

She gave me a patient smile. "I really have very little to do with all that. Someone looks after it for me. If there is something wrong with your house, I'll be happy to give you the agent's name and number."

"See," I bulled right on, "it's going to be knocked

down. Maybe you didn't know that. They are going to put a hotel there."

"Oh yes," she said. "I know. I'm the one who's doing it." She said it so casually, as if she were playing a game of Monopoly.

"Could you tell me what the problem is?" she said. "I'm in the midst of doing something."

"I wish you wouldn't, that's all," I said.

"Wouldn't what?"

"Tear it down."

She looked at me, clearly puzzled. I went on fast. "See, we've been going there for so many years. And I really like it. It's a great spot and . . ." I could hear myself, and I sounded like an escapee from Graham Cracker School. I felt like a fool.

"Did your parents tell you to come here?" she asked. I wasn't sure if she was amused or not.

"Oh no," I said quickly. "No, I stayed out here alone. My idea. They'd really be mad if they knew what I was doing. I just wanted to speak to you. I don't want it to happen."

"I am interested," she said. "But I'm in the midst of painting. Perhaps, sometime, when I have a moment . . ." I must have looked upset or something because she changed her mind and pulled the door open. "Why don't you come in?" she said. "If you don't mind talking while I work, and if it doesn't take too long."

The inside of her house wasn't at all what I had expected from the outside. I thought it would be old and fussy. Actually, it was all new, modern, more like a science-fiction movie than anything I had ever seen before.

The walls and ceiling were completely white. There wasn't much furniture, but what there was was smooth and bright with lots of sharp corners. On the walls were paintings, not *of* anything, but great blobs of bright colors, lines, and squares. She was big on squares. The whole house was like that. Her being anything but ancient made me feel a whole lot better right away.

She led me to the back of the house and into the room where she was working. It was completely different from the rest of the house. In the middle was this big easel with a painting on which she was working. It was like one of the paintings in the house—not of anything, mostly colors, shapes. Next to it was a kind of high table with lots of paint, tubes of paint. One side of the room had other paintings, but you could only see their backs.

On another wall was a huge bulletin board with lots of things tacked on it—pictures, words, sketches, bits of things. There was even a snakeskin.

I liked the place, and her too.

"Hope you don't mind my working," she said.

"No, it's interesting," I said, watching as she went up to her easel and stared at what she was doing as if I wasn't there.

I was hoping she'd start to paint, but instead she turned around and said, "Now tell me about your problem."

"It's like I said," I began, feeling better and better. "I was hoping to talk you out of building the hotel there. It's really nice the way it is now. A hotel would ruin it."

She considered what I said for a moment, and I had the feeling she had listened. Then she said, "Ruin it for whom?"

"Well," I stumbled, "for us, I guess."

"You and your parents?"

"I suppose."

She picked up a brush. "I agree with you about the East Neck," she said. "It is one of the nicest places on the island. I'm glad you see that. But a hotel would mean that lots of people could enjoy it. What about that?"

I had to admit that I hadn't thought of it that way. "Well," I tried, "usually hotels are ugly."

She gave me a warm smile. "What if I built a nice one?"

"Yeah, but . . ." was the best answer I could come up with.

"Actually," she continued, becoming serious, "I think you're right. Hotels are not generally attractive. That's why I've gone to a lot of trouble to get a very fine architect. It won't be a bad job. The truth is, though," she went on, "and I think you're old enough to understand this, there's a more important reason for building it."

"What's that?" I wanted to know.

"You're not from the island," she said, putting down her brush, "so you should know that summer people and natives look at things differently. Local people want that hotel. It'll bring more summer people, lower taxes, give jobs, enhance their quality of life. Not so bad, is it?"

"I don't know," I admitted, caught off guard by what she was saying.

"Try to see it from their point of view, Owen. You're bright. There aren't many people here. Still, they don't have an easy life. Anything that helps bring change can't be all bad, don't you think? Now you're a thoughtful person. Have you considered the possibility that you've only been thinking of yourself?"

Not expecting to have things turned on me, I began to get angry. "Why can't you build it here?" I said. "Where your house is?"

She laughed. "Owen, this house is almost two hundred years old. Even if I wanted to build here, I couldn't. It's on the National Historical Register. Since you're interested in saving lovely places, don't you think we should preserve our heritage?"

"I guess that's the way I feel about my house," I said.

She gave me her warm smile. "Owen," she said softly, "it's not yours. It's mine. But I don't even remember it. What does it look like?"

"I like it," was all I could say.

"But you're the only people there," she said. "Is that fair?"

I didn't know what to say. I just felt stupid. And I didn't think she was really answering me.

When I didn't say anything, she said, "Have I answered all your questions?"

"But you're doing it to make money, aren't you?" I finally got the nerve to say. "I mean, you'll make a lot. And the whole island will change. Not just there."

"I do hope it will make money," she agreed. "It's costing a very great deal to put up. Owen," she said, "I really admire your coming here to talk to me like this. You've got a lot of courage."

I stood there, getting angrier and angrier.

"I mean that," she continued. "Not many kids your age would stand up and talk the way you have. How old are you?"

"Fourteen."

"I'm even more impressed," she said with a smile. "You look older."

"If you *couldn't* make money on it," I said, "would you do it—for all those other reasons?"

"I suppose I should say yes," she admitted. "But the world doesn't let you do things that way. I'm not a charity." She turned back to her painting.

"Guess you won't change your mind then, will you?" I said, feeling it had all been a waste of time.

She gave me her big smile. "Did you really think a talk like this would make me change my mind?"

"I hoped so," I said.

"Things don't work that way," she said and started to paint.

I took a breath. "I don't intend to move out," I said in nothing more than a whisper. "I don't."

"Owen," she said, going on with her painting, "I'm a firm believer in people doing what they have to do. I really am. I admire it. Up to a point. Don't do anything foolish. Some things just aren't worth it. You can get knocked around." She turned to give me her pretty smile. "Are we still friends?"

"I'd better go," was my answer.

"Come back and tell me if the hotel isn't beautiful when it's up," she said. "It really will be. Take my word for it. Trust me. And I've enjoyed talking to you."

I turned around and headed out the front door, wanting to get back to my side of the island and look over the bay.

☀ A Memory of the Fifth Summer

The three of them—Alice, Pete, and Owen—had gone sailing in the bay. Alice, who was the eldest and the most experienced sailor, was at the tiller. Pete was sitting low by the centerboard. Nine-year-old Owen, stationed in front of the mainsail, had no task and could content himself with looking.

It had been a beautiful day; the hot August sun beat down, while high curling clouds were nothing more than backdrop to brilliant sky and dark water. The breeze had been bright. The boat, rented for the three weeks, ran easily. Silence; broken by the slap of the bow on the water, the hum of the stays that supported the mast, the slight flutter of the sails, the teasing quality of a dream sliding past.

Owen looked back. His brother, his face tilted to the sun, was toasting himself. Alice, straw hat on her head, was resting easy, her hand shifting back and forth with lazy confidence, keeping the boat running smoothly. She smiled warmly at him.

Owen could see both the mainland and Grenlow's Island; he even fancied he could see their house.

And then the wind vanished. Owen didn't realize it at first. It was the disappearance of the sounds that made him notice.

"Coming about," he heard Alice call as she attempted to tack and catch some wind. Instead, the boom rattled, the sails shook. In moments they had all but stopped.

For a while no one said anything.

"We're drifting," Peter announced.

"The wind will be back," said Alice.

Owen, for no reason, grinned back at his brother and sister.

"How's it going, Captain?" Alice called to him.

"Fifteen men on a dead man's chest," he shouted back.

"Want to steer?" she called.

"Later."

For perhaps ten minutes they floated peacefully. Then, since Owen was up front, he saw it first. "What's that?" he called out, pointing out over the water.

"Where?" asked Peter, twisting about.

"There," insisted Owen.

Out over the bay, in front of them, was what looked like a ballooning mist, a gray blot that seemed alive. Everything else was blue and green.

Pete stood up. "I don't know. What is it, Alice?"

Alice, taking her hand from the tiller, also stood.

As the boat rocked, Owen felt a twinge of nervousness. "What is it?" he wanted to know.

Alice stared at the ball of fog. "Could be a squall," she said softly.

Owen looked around. He didn't know the word. "Is a squall bad?"

Alice didn't answer. Instead, she sat down quickly and gripped the tiller. There was a look of puzzlement and worry on her face. Peter waited for her to say something.

In a matter of moments it grew cooler, almost cold. The surface of the water began to swell, as if something alive were rolling about beneath the water.

"Is it all right?" Owen called out, his voice sounding his worry.

"Sure," said Alice, but her eyes were fixed hard on the fog, which loomed larger. Abruptly she called to Pete, "Bring the sail down, quick!" The heaviness of her voice filling Owen with alarm.

Pete sprang up, and working as fast as possible, lowered the mainsail. Scrambling forward past Owen, almost pushing him aside, he started on the jib.

"Leave it!" commanded Alice.

Owen, without being asked, crawled back down

54

into the cockpit of the boat. There he sat, chin resting on his knees, which he clasped tightly.

The squall hit them.

It came in a fist of wind, first flinging rain, then throwing it, and finally dumping it. Alice swung the boat about, hoping to run before the weather. The boat heeled far over to one side. To Owen's horror, he saw a trickle of bay water thread into the boat like an unraveling string. They were that close to capsizing.

Alice's maneuver had been just fast enough. As quickly as the boat had heeled, it righted itself and leaped forward, moving as if propelled by a slingshot. Owen listened to the long hiss of the hull as it cut through the water, the cracking smack of the bow as it dipped and rose, dipped and rose.

Owen kept his eyes on Alice. Her hat had blown away, and her eyes squinted against the rain. Her mouth was tightly closed.

"Alice!" cried Owen.

"It's O.K., Owen," she called back to him, even making herself smile. Her hands—both of them on the tiller—were white from the tightness by which she clung on.

Pete, scrambling down the length of the boat, kneeled by the centerboard again, ready to do as he was told. He looked frightened.

No one said anything. Both Peter and Owen kept their eyes on Alice.

"It's O.K.," she said again. "Don't worry. They don't last long."

They were all soaked, streaming wet, and somehow seemed to be getting wetter. The water streaming over Owen's face was bitter with salt.

"Better get the bilge pump out," Alice shouted at Pete.

Without a word, his lips pursed, Pete crawled forward, pulled up the pipelike pump, and made it ready.

Owen dared not take his eyes from his sister. She made a kissing motion at him with her mouth, and he felt better.

They were racing faster and faster. Owen had never moved so fast in a boat.

"Where are we going?" he called out to Alice.

"Home," she said.

"Good," he replied, as much to himself as to her. "I don't think I like this."

The way he said it made her give a real smile, but the smile quickly faded.

Owen closed his eyes and tried to picture the house, and better than that, his room. How he wished he were there, wishing it more than anything!

Opening his eyes, he looked at Alice. Her hair, soaking wet, stuck to her face, but she didn't bother to push it off. Both hands were still clinging to the tiller. Owen hoped she wouldn't break it in two.

And then, as fast as it had come, the wind lessened, the rain slacked off. Not daring to believe it, they waited. Owen, watching, saw his sister lick her lips and hastily push the wet hair from her face.

The boat rocked gently. Feeling brave, Owen stood up and looked over the bow, steadying himself with one hand. The ball of fog was thinning rapidly. Only in front of them did it look bad.

"Bye-bye, baby," said Pete, who was also standing, one hand on the mast.

As they watched, the squall, like some living thing, seemed to rise up into the air and pass over the land.

56

*To their astonishment they saw the land was the East
Neck and held their house.*

They cheered.

*"Owen," called Alice wearily, "do you want to
steer?"*

*Owen, brave captain of the ship, sailed home, the
most beautiful place in the whole wide world.*

As I stood in the water digging clams I was thinking so hard about so many things that I didn't notice
Terri till she was standing on the shore opposite me.

"Hi," she said.

Startled, I looked up.

She saw the bunch of clams I had flipped over on
the beach. "Nice clams," she said, gathering them
into a pile. "You going to make a chowder?"

"I don't know how," I told her. "Besides, I don't
have a pot. Eat them raw, I suppose."

She made a face. "I never learned to like them
raw," she said. "Everybody else does. My sister can
eat two dozen raw. All my family can. I don't like
them." She looked at me.

"Ed Bermoldi came into the store right after you
left," she went on. "The policeman," she added when
I didn't react. "He wanted to know if I had seen you
around. Said he got a call from your folks last night.
They want him to put you on the bus for the city."

I didn't say anything.

"Then he said that if I saw you, I was to tell you
that he needs to see you. He said he would come over
here."

"Is that why you came?" I asked her. "To warn
me?"

"Your phone is out of order."

"Yeah," I said, standing up from the water. My

hands and arms were streaked with the thick black muck that clams love to live in. "I spoke to Miss Devlin," I told her, trying not to react to what she had said about my going home.

"People say you can't talk to her."

"I did."

"What happened?"

"She was nice, nicer than I thought she'd be. Not that she'd listen. If you ask me, she's only trying to make a lot of money."

"She's got a lot," said Terri.

"She wants more then," I said. "You know what she said?"

Terri shook her head.

"She says she's doing it for the island people. She says *they* want it."

Terri studied one of the clams, picked it up, and began washing it off at the water's edge. She reminded me of a raccoon.

"It's true, sort of," she said at last. "People do want it."

"I don't."

"You don't live here."

"I do," I said, getting angry. "The hotel will ruin the whole place. The place is beautiful. It is! I told Miss Devlin I'm going to stay. I'm not letting them do it."

"What are you going to do about Ed putting you on the bus?"

I didn't say anything.

"You can't fight everyone," she said. "Do you know what people are saying about you?"

"What people?"

"In town. Everybody."

"How do they know what I'm doing?"

"You can't keep things like that from them," said Terri. "Not here. They're really upset. They don't understand what you're doing. They think you might, you know, really do something."

"Like what?"

"Like keep the hotel from going up."

"They really do?"

"Yes." She looked at me. "What are you going to do now?" she asked.

"I don't know," I admitted. "I just don't know."

I was really upset, and it must have shown on my face.

"Maybe you should go home," she whispered.

I couldn't speak. I just shook my head.

"You should hear my brother," she said. "I mean, people are really worried. You don't understand what the hotel means to them."

"I live here!" I shouted.

"It's not as if you didn't try," Terri offered. "I mean, that was pretty good, going to talk to Miss Devlin like that. No one here would ever do that. It's making people nervous."

"They don't have to worry. She didn't listen."

"I know, but . . ." She gave up.

I didn't want to talk about it anymore, so I washed myself off. "I better get these clams home," I said.

I gathered up the clams, and we started toward the house. The September sun was very yellow, but the clouds overhead, thickening, seemed lower than usual.

"Supposed to rain tomorrow," she said.

"Good," I said. "They won't knock the place down." As we got closer to the house I examined it, trying to see it the way others did. "Do you think it's so bad?" I asked Terri.

She didn't say anything.

"Is it?" I insisted.

"It must have been nice when it was built," she finally said.

"What about now?"

"I guess—I don't think it's so great," she said, stressing the "so," and quickly adding, "but I don't know much about things like that."

I looked at the house again. "Maybe you're right," I said after a moment. "It doesn't look so great. Maybe if I fixed it up, people would see it differently, more the way I do."

She stopped and looked at it, then at me. "What could you do?"

I didn't have any real ideas, not then. "Just a thought," I had to say.

We went into the house and put the clams in the sink where I began to wash away the rest of their mud.

"What happened to your phone?" she asked. "The phone company said something was wrong."

"I ripped it out."

"How come?"

"My parents were bugging me."

"You do whatever you want, don't you?" she said.

I didn't say anything to that.

Then she said, "I have to go home. My school starts tomorrow."

"Right," I said.

She hesitated by the door. "Why don't you make a fire on the beach and make the clams that way? You can do potatoes too."

"I don't have any potatoes."

"If you could wait," she said, "I could probably sneak some out to you."

"No, that's all right," I told her. "I've got enough."

"Give me two hours," she said, and I saw she really wanted to.

"O.K. with me," I said. "I'll get a fire going."

"See you," she called and hurried out the door.

As she went I watched, trying to decide exactly what I thought of her. I figured she must like me or she wouldn't have bothered to come in the first place. I wondered what she would do if I tried to touch her.

I scrubbed the clams furiously, then felt hungry. I finished off the rest of the peanut butter, did some eyebrow practice, then went out to get some wood for the fire.

When I finally got enough, I lit some of it with my father's butane lighter. It wasn't a very big fire, but I didn't want to use the wood too fast. Then I sat before it, watching, throwing in bits of wood, thinking about what Terri had said and about what the house used to look like.

☀ A Memory of the First Summer

"Where is it?" Owen kept asking, squirming out of the protective arms of his mother and pressing forward to look out the front window of the car. "Where is it?"

"Be patient, Owen," his mother suggested, knowing it was useless to suggest patience to a five-year-old. "We're almost there."

No one was being patient. In the back seat Owen's brother and sister were leaning forward too, each eager to claim the prize for being the first one to see the summer cottage their parents had rented. Mr. and

Mrs. Coughlin kept exchanging looks, smiling, laughing. They were excited too.

"Just remember, kids," Mr. Coughlin was saying, "it's not ours. We're only renters. We have to be careful with things, especially if we want to come back next year."

"Is that it?" Peter cried out as they passed a house.

"I told you," said Mrs. Coughlin. "It's alone on a beach, and it's just a little place."

The car swung out of the bend. Unexpectedly they were moving free of trees, the bay on one side, sky everywhere.

Alice saw it first. "There it is!" She screamed.

Owen, who had been frantic to find it, searched wildly about but could see nothing. "Where? Where?" he cried.

They were racing along the beach road now, and as Owen swiveled about he saw a small white building. "Is that it?" he asked his mother quietly, as if it were a thing too fragile to say out loud.

"Yes," she said into his ear.

Mr. Coughlin drew the car to the top of the driveway. They barely came to a stop when the back doors flung open and Pete and Alice leaped from the car and began to run down the driveway.

Owen, desperate to get out, groped for the door handle. Mrs. Coughlin, laughing, opened the door for him, and Owen all but tumbled to the ground.

Picking himself up, he ran to the top of the driveway, then stopped. The house, glistening white, astonished him. It was there, alone, unattached, unsupported. Sand lay on one side, endless water on the other. It was like nothing he had ever seen with his own eyes before, more like something in a picture.

His mother came to stand beside him. Reaching for her hand, Owen squeezed it.

"Is that where we're going to live?" he asked.

"That's it."

"For ever and ever?" he asked.

"Just for three weeks, Owen."

"Then what?" he wanted to know.

"Then you start your new school back in the new city."

He drew her closer to her. "Mommy, do you know what?"

"What's that, Owen?"

"If we wanted to, we could just live here."

"Would you like that?"

"Yes."

"Why?"

Owen studied the house again and tried to fit together the feelings that seemed to come and go as incomplete pictures.

"Because," he said at last. "There's no one else to take care of the house, and it wants us to."

His mother hugged him hard.

I kept wishing I knew what time it was, feeling pretty sure that two hours had passed and that Terri wasn't going to come. It made me feel more isolated than ever. I was also starving, and in spite of myself I kept wondering what my folks might have left for my dinner that night. As it was, I had this notion that they would suddenly show up and force me back to the city. For a decent hamburger, I might have considered it.

That made me think about my not going to school, which I knew could cause trouble. Still, I figured the school couldn't do much. It wasn't as if I had a record of making trouble anywhere.

Last spring I had visited the school I was supposed to start. Where I had been going before had been big, but this place was huge. And the kids seemed much older. I hadn't felt so young in a long time.

I didn't like what I saw. I met this counselor—a Mr. Matlock—who looked like a pro football center. This guy—someone told me he was known as "Meathook"—spent five minutes laying down a million rules. The next five minutes he spent telling me they had decided I was going to be a top student.

Either way it sounded like a threat, and I was glad I wasn't there.

I flipped over on my side, feeling cold on one half of me, warm on the other. An occasional puff of wind caused the flames to die down, only to flare up again.

That was the way I was feeling.

The fact is I wasn't feeling good with the way things were happening. I mean, I couldn't help but think about what Miss Devlin had said. I didn't like it. I didn't even think she had answered me and didn't believe she was building the hotel for the reasons she gave.

Still, it kept crawling into my mind that maybe she was right, that when I put all those people against me and what I wanted, I didn't come off too great. When I added what Terri had said—how people were so upset about my staying—it got worse. Then there were my parents.

It all kept nagging at me. What if everybody else was right and I was wrong? What was so important to me, I mean *really* important? I wasn't sure I could answer.

Restless, I got up, walked around, wishing that Terri would come. It was getting dark.

I couldn't help myself; the more I thought about things, the worse I felt. Maybe, I told myself, I should just get out and go home. It would be easier.

I moved up a-ways to see if she was coming, but saw no sign. Then I made myself sit down. I thought about her again, wondering whether or not she was pretty. I couldn't make up my mind about that either. I asked myself if she liked me. In the back of my mind was this notion that she was only hanging around because her parents told her to.

When I couldn't wait any longer, I jumped up and went to get the clams. As I did, I heard a sound on the driveway. I stopped and looked around, seeing only a small glowing light. Right away I got worried, thinking how Terri had warned me about people not liking me.

"Terri?" I called softly.

"Hi," she called back, flicking off her bike light.

As she came around the house I saw she was carrying a bag.

"Sorry I'm late," she said. "I couldn't get away right off. I had to tell them I was going somewhere else. I've got a nosy brother." She held out the bag. "Potatoes. And ketchup for the clams. Makes them taste better."

"Great," I said, suddenly feeling free again. "See if the fire's big enough. I'll get the clams." I ran to the house, excited.

I came out a few minutes later. I had turned off the house lights and had managed to gather up all the clams. Back at the fire, Terri had already put the potatoes in and was sitting back, watching them, her arms wrapped around her. Looking at her, I decided she was pretty.

"Now what?" I asked, dumping the pile carefully on the sand in front of her.

She picked up one of the clams. "If you put them around so that they don't spill when they open, they're even better," she explained. With a deft movement she flipped the largest clam right into the fire's edge. The flame sputtered, the shell began to blacken.

One by one I handed her the clams. She put each clam around the fire until they made a complete circle.

"Now what?" I asked.

"You'll see. They cook fast." She sat back, hands wide to her side.

I sat nearby. Even as I did, the first of the clams, like an opening fist, sputtered and yawned open.

"See," she said. "Fast."

"Great," I said. The smell was fantastic.

"The potatoes take longer. Maybe an hour."

We sat watching. I became aware of how close her hand was to mine.

"Now," she said suddenly, "get the cap off the ketchup and pour some into each open clam. Then cook them a little more."

I did as she told me.

The smell got even better, but still we sat back and waited. Then Terri said, "Go on, eat the first one."

I didn't need to be told twice. The clams were really bubbling. I got two sticks and managed to maneuver that first big clam out. When I got it out, I tried to grab it with my hand, but it was too hot.

After poking it around till it cooled down a bit, I took it up. Pulling the shell apart, I used one shell side as a spoon to scoop out the meat. I offered it to Terri.

"No," she said, laughing. "You first."

I stuffed the clam into my mouth with my fingers. It was chewy, a little too hot, but fantastic. As I sucked in some air to cool it, juice dribbled down my chin.

"What do you think?" she asked anxiously.

"Great," I sputtered, my mouth still full. "Go on. You take one."

I think we ate all the clams in fifteen minutes. She had two. I had the rest and could have eaten more.

"Best clams I ever ate," I told her, wiping my fingers on my jeans. Then I sat back, poking the fire. Even as I did so I stole a look at Terri, trying to decide what had worried me before.

"Can I ask you something?" I finally said.

"I guess so."

"Don't get mad. I just need to know."

She waited.

"What I mean is, it's all your help, and being nice and all that. . . . Did my parents ask you to, you know, make sure I was all right or something? I mean, are you doing all this because they asked you to?"

"No." It was all she said. I could tell she didn't like being asked that, and I was sorry right off that I had asked. I tried to think of something else fast, but couldn't.

She kept her silence, and I kept wishing I knew what she was thinking. I mean, I felt I had to do *something,* touch her, maybe even kiss her. But I didn't know how to start.

"What are you going to do?" she asked me.

For a second I thought she was reading my mind. "About what?" I managed to say.

"Yourself," she said, dead serious. "Are you going to leave?"

I was so tired of being asked that. "I guess my staying is a waste of time," I said after a moment.

She looked away, and I had the feeling she hadn't wanted me to say that either.

"I mean," I tried to explain, "I thought I could do something, thought it was a good idea. Nobody else seems to think it's important." I was hoping she would say it was.

All she said was, "They don't see it the way you do."

I shrugged. "I tried telling Miss Devlin, didn't I? She's the only one who counts around here. I suppose if the place were all fixed up, you know, the way her place is, it might be different. You should see her house. Wild. Not what you'd expect. If I had her kind of money, I could fix up this place. Least, fix it up enough to make her notice, to make her think it was beautiful. But," I admitted, "I can't do anything."

"I thought you could," said Terri sadly.

The way she said that made me even more depressed.

I was trying to get up the nerve to tell her I was going to leave when I heard her say, "Do you know what *I* want? Want more than anything?"

"No," I said, looking up.

"You don't know what this island is like," she said. "It's so much the same. Every day. Nothing happens. Nothing changes. I sometimes think . . ." She stopped and took a deep breath. "I sometimes think," she said again, "that if I saw something, something beautiful, *really* beautiful—I don't even know what it would be—but if I did see it, then, well, maybe, *I* could do something different—for myself."

"I don't understand," I said.

"I said you should leave this afternoon," she said quietly.

"I know."

"I don't want you to," she said so softly that for a second I thought she was crying. "I suppose you should leave, but I don't want you to."

I didn't know what to say. She wouldn't even look at me. "I did have one idea," I said after a while.

"What?"

"About the house. Remember you said how it didn't look so great?"

"I don't know—"

"Maybe," I said, "what I should do is fix it up, do something different."

She looked at me then. She *had* been crying.

"You know," I said, "something crazy. Something, beautiful, maybe." The idea excited me. "Houses don't have to be white, or even one color. Different colors." I was beginning to feel excited. "Hey," I called out. "Polka dots. Something wild like that."

She laughed.

"With special lights," I went on, the idea becoming more and more fun. "Weird, strange-looking windows. Nothing square. Why do windows always have to be square? Anything but square."

"It would be different," she agreed.

"Boy," I said, pictures coming one after the other into my head. "I'd like to do that."

"I know where there's some paint," said Terri.

It was as if she were challenging me. "You're kidding. Where?"

"At Bateman's Boat Yard," she said. "Summer

people fix up their boats—painting and stuff. A lot of them leave the leftover paint. Different colors. My brother used to get some."

"Could we?"

"I think so."

"Hey, right!" I cried, becoming more and more caught up in the thing. "Make the place so fantastic that, you know, newspapers, the TV, everybody would see it. A national monument. Just like Miss Devlin's house. Really important. They would just—" I never finished.

"Hey, look at this cute party." A voice spoke from the edge of the dark.

We spun around. It was her brother Bill and two of his friends.

For a moment, nobody said anything. Terri and I stared up at the three intruders. I recognized Bill but not the other two.

It was Terri who spoke first. "What is it, Bill?" she asked, her voice tiny. "What is it?"

"Nothing," he said. "I just wanted to see how things are going. Couple of sweeties."

His two friends laughed.

"What are you going to do?" asked Terri.

"I said, nothing. I just wanted to make sure he's treating you right. He bothering you or anything?"

"No."

"That's good," Bill said to her. "If he puts a finger on you, a *finger,* I'm going to bust him in the mouth."

One of his friends murmured his approval.

"In fact," Bill continued to Terri, "I think you'd better go home. This kid and I are going to have a talk. Isn't that right?" he said, turning to face me for the first time.

I wanted to say something but couldn't get any

words out. Still sitting, I looked up at the three across the fire, knowing that I was really scared.

"Bill," tried Terri. "I don't think—"

"You've got school tomorrow, Terri. Take off. You're not even supposed to be here. Want me to tell Mom? You said you were going to Angela's. Now go."

For a moment Terri stood where she was, unsure what to do. She kept looking from her brother to me.

"Go on, beat it," her brother demanded.

With a timid gesture she turned toward me, and lifting a hand said, "Good-bye." Then she hurried away.

I didn't see her go. My eyes were on Bill.

He kept looking down at me. One of the others circled around to stand between me and the water. I wouldn't be able to get away in that direction.

"Don't you think you'd better stand when you talk to your elders, kid?" said Bill when he was sure Terri had gone.

My heart pounding, I somehow got up.

Bill came around the fire, close to me, touching me lightly on the chest. "What we want to know, kid, is two things. First, what are you mucking around with Terri for?"

"I'm not," I managed to get out, sensing how silly it sounded. "We're just friends."

"Friends," echoed Bill, forcing himself to laugh. The two others laughed in chorus. "Let me tell you something. You keep away from her. *Keep away.* Don't come near her. Don't even come near the store!" he suddenly shouted. "I don't care what you want. You can't get anything there. You understand?"

"What is it?" I got myself to say. "Just tell me what it is."

"That's the second point," said Bill. "When the hell are you getting off this island, getting off and going back where you belong?

"The season's over," he shouted, getting angrier all the time. "You're all done here. You're gone. Out. We want you out!"

"This is our place," I whispered, backing up a step.

"The hell it is," cried Bill. "It's coming down, understand. This thing is coming down if I have to rip it down myself. And you know why it's coming down? Because we don't like it. We've got something better to put here. I just want to know when you're getting out."

I shook my head.

Instantly, Bill's hand shot out and shoved me hard on the shoulder, making me spin about. Arms flying wildly, I stumbled down on one knee.

Trying hard to keep from crying, I repeated the words, "I'm not going."

It was as if he wouldn't believe what I was saying. He stepped back and looked at his friends, then looked at me. The other two were grinning. Not knowing what to do, I waited for him to hit me again.

"Go on," called one of his friends. "Show him what you mean."

"Hear what they're saying?" Bill shouted, getting angrier and angrier. "They want an answer too. *When are you going?*"

I shook my head again.

"Come on, Bill, show him what you can do," one of the others called out.

Bill took a step toward me. "Get up," he yelled.

Too scared to stand, I slumped down.

"Get up," shouted Bill as he grabbed my arm, pulling me up. "Look, kid," he tried, "I didn't come here to punch you out, just to get you out. But you're asking for it. You are asking for it." His hand was trembling as he pointed at me.

I could hardly look at him.

"Damn it!" he screamed. "Give me an answer."

"I'm not going," I managed to say again.

"O.K., O.K.," said Bill, backing off. "That's you saying it. Now you're going to have to fight. Now you're going to have to. Not all of us. Oh no, not all. Pick the one you want. Go on, pick."

I looked at them. The only light was from the fire, and it made their faces flat, orange-red, their mouths gaping.

"I don't want to fight," I said, trying to move away.

Someone blocked me.

"Go on, kid," demanded Bill, "Pick. Hey, Mike," he called, grabbing one of his friends and shoving him forward. "Mike's the smallest. Go on, Mike," he said, almost throwing him at me. "Mike's a runt like you," and he slapped his friend on the back.

Mike, laughing, suddenly reached out and struck me across the face with his fingertips.

It didn't hurt so much as it surprised me.

"Hey!" shouted the others. "You see that. Slapped him on the face. Hey, slapped him!"

"Come on, kid," taunted Mike. "Fight me!" He was holding his arms by his side, his face leaning forward, daring me to hit him back. "Fight me!" he yelled, dancing up and down. Then he hit me again. I tried to dodge it, but he caught me on the ear.

When he hit me that way, the second time, it was like pulling a trigger. I leaped at him, screaming, throwing my hands at him.

It caught him completely off guard. And when,

73

like a wild man, I just went at him—not even knowing what I was doing—he tried to back off, only to trip and fall to the sand. I dropped right on him, hitting him, kicking him.

The others started to cheer, but when they saw I was getting the best of it, they jumped in too.

I didn't feel a thing. I just kept striking out at everything, hearing only my own screams. "I'm staying! I'm staying!"

All of a sudden a new voice burst in. "All right! All right!" it said. "Break it up!"

I felt bodies go slack and roll off, leaving me alone on the sand.

"You out of your minds?" I heard the voice ask. With my arms over my face for self-protection, I couldn't see who was talking. When I did move, a bright light blinded me.

Bill was saying, "He jumped us, Ed. He really did, didn't he?"

"Dirty fighter," said one of the others. They were standing on the far side of the fire.

Mr. Bermoldi squatted down beside me, calling Terri to bring the lighter closer. "How you doing?" he said.

I pushed myself up and tried to look around. My head throbbed. Wet dribbled down my chin. I felt like spitting. When I wiped the wet off, it was slippery. In the light I could see it was blood. Then I began to feel the pain.

"Terri said these guys jumped you," Bermoldi was saying. "That right?"

I nodded.

"The hell we did!" Bill cried out. "We were only talking to him. Doing nothing, Ed, just talking. He jumped us. He's crazy. Some queer."

"What happened?" Bermoldi, still by my side, asked me.

I sniffed, trying to clear my nose. I felt awful, embarrassed, stupid. "They came here," I said. "First he told me to, uh, leave Terri alone. Then he told me—to get off the island." I took a few gulps of air. It was hurting to talk. "When I said I wouldn't, he said I had to fight one of them."

"That's a load of crap!" cried Bill.

"Go on," said Bermoldi.

"I didn't want to fight," I said. "I didn't. Then one of them—"

"Which one?" Bermoldi asked, moving his light so that I could look at them. The three were standing side by side.

"That one," I said. "The one on the end."

"What did he do?"

"Hit me. Twice."

"Bull!" raged Mike. "Hey, Ed, who you gonna believe, him or me? He's making it up."

"Then what happened?" Bermoldi said to me.

"I don't know," I admitted. "I got mad. Lost my temper. Started to swing at him. Then they all jumped me."

Bermoldi looked over my face again, then stood up. From where I was, he looked huge.

"You going to believe him or us?" demanded Mike.

"Get up to your car," Bermoldi ordered. "And wait there for me. *Wait*. Understand?"

"Hey, come on," tried Bill.

"Get going!" roared Bermoldi.

"Come on," said Mike as the three of them marched off.

Bermoldi watched them for a moment, then looked

down at me. "Can you stand up?" he asked, holding out a hand.

I took it, and he hauled me up. I was hurting all over.

"Give me the light, Terri," said Bermoldi. He held it close to my face. "You're not going to look like a movie star tomorrow," he said. "Can you walk?"

I took a few steps. I could manage.

"O. K.," said Bermoldi. "Now listen to me. I know what happened. Terri told me how it started. The only reason I'm here is because I got another call from your parents. They want to know what's going on. I was coming here to ask you that question when I met Terri on the road. She got me here a little quicker."

For the first time I looked around to see where Terri was. She was standing by the low fire, looking small, frightened, staring at me. I tried to nod to her and wasn't sure if I managed it. Believe it or not, the thought came to me that I should try to raise the one eyebrow.

"What happened to your phone?" Bermoldi asked.

"I ripped it out."

"Why?"

I couldn't explain.

"Look, kid," said Bermoldi. "Don't worry about those guys. Nothing like that is going to happen again. *Nothing.* I promise you. If they so much as look at you funny, I want to know about it. I'm sorry it happened. I really am. Now, promise to let me know."

I nodded.

"Hey, now, what I really need to know is, what are you doing? How long do you intend to hang around?"

I couldn't believe it. It was the same question that everybody asked.

"You're supposed to be in school, aren't you?"

I closed my eyes. What I really wanted to do was sleep.

"Owen," said Bermoldi, "I could put you on the bus tomorrow. You know that, don't you?"

I nodded.

"I'd rather you do it yourself," he said softly. "Hey, what do you say?"

I opened my eyes and looked past him, at Terri. She was watching me intently. When I turned back to Bermoldi, I could see the muscles tighten around his jaw.

After what had happened, after what Terri had said to me before, I couldn't give up. I didn't even want to.

"Do you know when they're supposed to tear the building down?" I asked, trying to find a way to stall.

"I'll find out," he said.

"I need to know," I said.

"Good enough," said Bermoldi. "Hey, want to come over to my place tonight? Take a shower? Fix up your face? You'll sleep better, and it will help you see your way clear."

I shook my head. "I want to stay here."

"Sure?"

I nodded.

Bermoldi looked at me carefully, then accepted it. "I'll come by in the morning to see if everything is the way it should be. I'll have your answer too, right?" He put his hand on my shoulder and gave it a little shake. "Hey, you did O.K. Us off-islanders, we do all right, eh?"

Then he turned. "We'd better go, Terri." He went up the driveway, taking the flashlight with him.

I could feel myself swaying on my feet.

Terri was still there. "I'm sorry," she said.

"Wasn't anything you did."

Behind us, up on the road, I could hear voices, mostly Bermoldi's.

"They won't bother you anymore," said Terri. "They're scared of him."

"So am I," I said.

Terri crossed her arms over her chest. "I guess I'd better go," she said. "I shouldn't have come back either." There were tears on her face.

I looked at her.

"Just makes trouble," she said. "People getting hurt."

I was listening, trying hard to get my feelings into one place. I couldn't. But I knew that what she was saying was wrong. "If you can get it," I said, "I'd like that paint. You said you knew where to get it."

"Terri!" It was Bermoldi calling. "Come on!"

"Please," I said. "I want that paint."

"I'll try to get it," she said. "After school."

"Terri!"

"I have to go," she said, as if I couldn't understand what was happening. Then, and I wasn't expecting it, she came up to me and with a clumsy reach kissed me on the side of the face. She moved away, not looking back.

At my feet only clumps of hot coals, glowing on and off, were left from the fire. The breeze off the bay made me feel cold. I felt sick. Still, I stood there, making myself wait until the cars went. It was important to me that they leave first.

When they did, I collapsed. Down on my hands

and knees I went and just puked. Then, mostly crawling, I made my way back to the house and onto my bed. The smell of the house, just the way it gave out with its regular creaks and squeaks, made me feel better. And I wasn't crying. I wasn't. I wasn't going to give them that.

What was the worst, and it really was worse than anything, was that I had almost said I would leave. That hit me in the head again and again. I felt like a traitor. But I knew I didn't want to quit. Not then, not anymore. Even if it was wrong to stay, I had to stay. I had to.

No matter what happened.

Wednesday

*I*n the morning I ached all over. My left shoulder was sore, my mouth felt as if it were stuffed with cotton, my ribs pinched with every breath. When I put my hand to my lip, I found it puffed. Fortunately, it was gray outside or my eyes would have hurt.

For a while I was glad to lie in bed, going over what had happened the night before, wondering if I had been brave or a coward. In the end I decided that while I hadn't been exactly great, and that when I went crazy I hadn't really known what I was doing, I had done O.K. I hadn't just stood there. Almost, not quite.

I thought about Terri a lot. And about that kiss she had given me. In spite of myself I grinned. It hurt my mouth.

I dozed some more. When I awoke, the room seemed darker. For a moment I thought I had actually slept through the day.

Pushing myself up, I looked out the window and saw heavy, low, fast-moving clouds. Then I became aware of how damp everything felt. It would be raining soon.

I went into the bathroom and studied myself in the mirror. I was startled. My upper lip was cut, and a deep blue and red patch was on my forehead. It took me a few moments to realize that the purple blot of color all around my right eye was a black eye. I had never seen one before. Now I had one of my very own.

I looked at my hands. They were scratched. A cuticle was torn, a nail broken.

The zit on the side of my nose was bigger, but I figured no one would bother to notice that now.

I stepped back to take a better look and tried to raise one eyebrow. It came up pretty easy, and for a moment I thought I had done it until I realized that it was mostly due to the lump over that eye.

Anyway, I decided I didn't look too bad, especially when I tried my half-smile, cocking my head to one side a bit.

"Owen!" someone called.

I really jumped.

"Owen!" came the call again. "It's Ed Bermoldi."

Relaxing, I shouted back, "Be right out."

Bermoldi was a big guy, and even though he wasn't so old, he was mostly bald. He was always in uniform, very neat. But he didn't look so great because he was pretty heavy and getting heavier. Also, he wore one of those belts with police stuff all over it—revolver, handcuffs, bullets. It made him look like a walking hardware store.

He was just standing there looking at the kitchen mess when I walked in. Seeing me, he did a real double-take.

"Hey," he said. "They really painted your face pretty, didn't they? You all right? You sleep O.K.? Lose any teeth? Tell you the truth, last night I didn't think you were this bad."

"I'm O.K."

He studied me for a moment. "Look," he said, "we better have a little talk. Mind if we sit?"

I led him into the main room. He lowered himself into a wicker chair, making it squeak. When he sat, he looked fatter than ever, his stomach rolling over his bullets, like one of those laughing Buddhas, only with a gun.

He placed his cap carefully on the table. "First things first," he began. "I got to admire what you're doing. Don't agree with it, but admire it. You know, I'm not from the island. And between you and me, these people, well, they don't like listening to outsiders like us. You know," he said, tapping his head, "hard as clams. But you and me, I think we're alike.

"That's the first thing. The second is this: Those guys won't bother you again. I meant what I said last night. Even if they trouble you a little bit, I want to hear about it. That clear?"

He paused before speaking again, and I had the feeling he was just getting to the important part.

Sure enough, he leaned forward and spoke more softly. "Going to get your parents to press charges?"

The thought had never occurred to me. "What do you mean?"

"Assault. Battery. Harassment. Conspiracy. Trespassing. Intentional infliction of emotional distress. Trespass to person. You name it, kid, you can do it. And I've got more if you want." He paused. "That is, if it's what you want your parents to do. Course, if *you* don't cooperate, they can't make a case. No way."

"I don't know," I said.

"Probably didn't even think about it, did you?" he said, sitting back, trying to smile.

"I just got up."

83

He leaned forward. "Look, it's not my place to give advice on something like this, so if you don't want it, I won't. But seeing as you and me are so much the same—"

"I'm listening."

"If I were you, I wouldn't press charges. I mean, don't get me wrong. Maybe they should be brought in. And if, like I said, they do something again, I'd *make* you bring charges. But, hey, figure it this way. You're going to be leaving soon." He stopped and looked at me. "That's what you said, right?" Without waiting for an answer, he went on. "So you'll be out of the picture. Besides, the only way you can really make the charges stick is by asking Terri to be a witness. Do you see the whole thing now?"

He pushed himself to the edge of his chair. "Hey, do you know why they pitched into you?"

"Terri?"

Bermoldi shook his head. "They're scared of you, Owen."

I looked at him, not believing.

"Maybe they don't even know it. But I'm telling you, that's what it is. Look," he said, "like I said, I'm not an islander. I see it. Island people think all summer people are rich."

"We're not," I let him know.

"And powerful," he continued. "For instance, here you're saying you're going to keep them from building the hotel."

"I wish I could."

"Hey, look, everybody knows what you're doing, buddy, or trying to do. Owen, do you have the smallest idea what that hotel means to the people here?" He answered his own question. "Jobs," he said. "Bill Janick, eighteen, and what does he do? He pumps gas

84

for his busted old man. If that hotel goes up, he might get a decent job."

"That's what Miss Devlin said."

"Hey, it doesn't matter to *me* if that hotel goes up. I can come or go. But to *them* . . . Owen, you might just stop it. They're afraid of you."

I was beginning to feel ill again.

"Before I came over," he said, "I checked out when this place is coming down."

I looked at him.

"Today is Wednesday. They come on Saturday. In three days, Owen, the tide comes in. No fooling. No way to stop it."

"Why do people think I can stop it?" I wanted to know.

"When you're scared, you can believe anything. Maybe you've never been scared."

"Do *you* think I can stop it?"

He sat back, eyes on my face. "Like I said, you never know. Maybe your old man's important, has connections."

"He's nobody."

Bermoldi grinned. "Hey, like the rest of us. Tell you what, Owen. Let me treat you to a ride on the bus on Friday. That way you won't have to watch them knock down the house."

I shook my head.

For the first time he showed annoyance. "Come on, buddy, you have to be reasonable too."

"You said I could stay until it came down, right?"

"Right."

"Well, *if* it comes down, I'll go."

"Saturday," he warned. "Saturday for sure."

"*If,*" I repeated.

He tapped his fingers on one knee. "Something

85

tells me you have an idea it won't happen. Want to let me in on it?"

I didn't say anything.

"Hey, I trust you," he said, and reached across with a large open hand. "It's a deal."

There wasn't anything I could do. I shook. He almost crushed my hand.

He stood up. "You going to tell your folks or should I?" he asked.

"My phone doesn't work," I reminded him.

"What about food? Got enough?"

"Sure."

He reached into his hip pocket and brought out a fat wallet, removing two five-dollar bills. "Your parents said I should give you this." He placed the money on the table. "That should see you through. You can ask for more." He started to go out, then stopped at the door. "What about the charges against those guys?"

"I guess I won't."

"You're smart," said Bermoldi. "And like I said last night, I think you've got a lot of guts. Now, keep loose," he said, and left.

Suddenly I remembered something and ran out after him. He was looking over the bulldozer.

"Mr. Bermoldi!" He looked up. "Terri and I," I started to say, feeling embarrassment. "Is it going to be, you know, bad for her if, well, we're still friends?"

"Hey," he called, grinning, "I'm engaged to her sister. If that family can get along with me, they'll be friends with anyone. Even you. Besides, I'm telling people you're going. See you!" With a final wave, he left.

After he had gone, I retreated to the kitchen for

something to eat, getting out the cold cereal and the milk. Naturally I didn't have a bowl. So I stuffed the flakes into my mouth with one hand and drank from the milk carton between mouthfuls.

Then I went outside. First I went to the spot where the fire had been. All that remained was a flat, gray circle of ash in the middle of which were lumps of blackened clam shells, potatoes, and the ketchup bottle. I stirred the mess around with my foot. Dead cold.

I studied it and thought it was looking the way I felt, only it was doing a better job of it.

Out back I looked at the bulldozer. It was there, like always. While I stood there, a faint drizzle started coming down. Its very softness got to me. I began to feel upset all over again, awfully tired, maybe even sick.

In my room I lay down and thought about the rain.

☀ A Memory of the Seventh Summer

Eleven-year-old Owen wasn't feeling well. His head ached, his stomach didn't seem right. Outside it looked the way he was feeling: rain all day with no hint of any letup.

"What should I do?" he asked his mother.

She looked up from the book she was reading. "Come read something next to me," she suggested.

He asked the same question of his father, who was on the front porch cleaning some of his fishing gear. "Help me if you'd like," he offered. "Plenty to do."

Alice was writing a long, long letter to a boy-friend. Pete was building a complicated model and told Owen to stop peering over his shoulder.

For a time Owen stayed in his room, lying on his bed and listening to the radio. It was boring. He went to the kitchen, made some cocoa, and stared out the back window.

It was from the kitchen that he saw the propane gas man. He didn't come very often. The propane gas came in heavy steel tanks that were plugged into the house out back, replaced, and carted off when empty. During the Coughlins' three-week stay, the gas man usually came once.

Instantly forgetting his boredom, Owen flew to get his raincoat and dashed outside to watch what the propane man was doing.

By the time he reached the place where the tanks were plugged in, Mr. Hinks, the gas man, wearing his bright yellow slicker against the rain, had lifted the steel hood off the old tank and was reading the meter. Owen stood close, observing.

Mr. Hinks nodded to him. "Morning," he called.

"Hi," said Owen.

"You don't mind the rain, do you?"

Owen just watched.

Mr. Hinks, after carefully jotting down the gauge reading in a little book, took out a special steel tool that turned the gas valves. It was long and flat, like a spoon, but with sockets on either end.

"Always a little left," he said. "Never can be safe enough. Don't want an explosion, do we?"

Owen, enthralled by the danger, watched, fascinated as Mr. Hinks fitted the special tool to the top of the tank and spun it around, shutting off the gas flow from the old tank.

"Wish my assistant didn't mind the rain," Mr. Hinks said to Owen. "He looks at the rain and decides he's a sugar plum, and might likely melt." Mr.

Hinks pulled the valve hard shut, then handed the tool to Owen. "Here, hold that, will you?"

Delighted to take part, Owen held the tool as the rain continued to pour down.

Mr. Hinks unfastened the coupling on the tank with three fast spins, then started to pull the tank. He stopped abruptly and looked at Owen. "You don't smoke, do you?" he asked.

"No," answered Owen seriously.

"Good thing too," said Mr. Hinks, continuing his operation. "Smoking and gas don't match." He looked slyly at Owen to see if the boy had caught the pun. "Match, get it?" he said. "That's all it takes and there she blows. Mind," he said, "propane is pretty safe. Self-contained. If she blows, she blows short and sweet. Not like line gas. You can't stop it then."

Easing the tank out, Mr. Hinks spun it around into a dolly next to the new tank. Then he took the new tank and swung it into position, fitted valve to valve. He asked for his special tool, and Owen handed it over.

Mr. Hinks fastened the coupling, then opened the valve. A momentary hiss could be heard. "There she goes, my boy. Plenty of hot tea for a cold day."

Mr. Hinks pulled the dolly toward his truck. Owen followed close behind. The loading was done quickly, and then the gas man asked for his tool.

As Owen handed it back, Mr. Hinks had a second thought. "I could use an assistant like you today. You doing anything? Got any jobs lined up?"

Owen shook his head.

"Go ask your folks if I can hire you for today. Two bucks fair and square?"

Thrilled, Owen ran for the house. Almost shouting, he asked his mother if he could go with Mr. Hinks, the propane man. She agreed, and an understanding was soon reached.

"Only one thing," said Mr. Hinks with a wink to Mrs. Coughlin. "He says he don't smoke. He telling the truth?"

"Far as I know," said Mrs. Coughlin.

"It's a deal then. In you go, my boy, in the truck. Now, hang on to that tool."

They worked until four o'clock, Mr. Hinks even treating Owen to a hamburger at Janick's. Mr. Hinks was full of disaster stories about fires, explosions, in particular gas explosions. They were quick and deadly, but with propane, not too bad. Owen, loving the details, listened intently.

At the end of the day Mr. Hinks insisted on paying Owen two dollars and fifty cents. "Good work gets good wages," he said, shaking Owen's hand like a man.

Mr. Hinks even praised Owen to his father. "Wish I could use him every day. Now just remember, boy, no smoking. Don't want any explosions. Bad publicity."

And he drove off.

Only later did Owen realize that he still had the special tool. Smoothing out the dollar bills, he wrapped his wages around the tool, putting both money and tool beneath his pillow. That night he slept the sleep of a workingman.

I slept most of the day. When I awoke, I looked outside. There was less rain, and I was hungry again.

There was hardly any food left, and the only place to buy anything was Janick's. I wondered if I should even go near. Bermoldi did say I wouldn't be bothered, but I couldn't be sure. Then I told myself that

I had already partly given in about leaving the island, that I shouldn't give in about other things. But most of all—and I knew it—I wanted to see Terri. So I pulled on a waterproof jacket, stuffed my money into a pocket, and started out, giving the bulldozer a dirty look as I went.

It was good to be outside. I didn't mind the rain. Everything was rich, glowing, misty; it gave me the feeling that I was looking at the world through velvet eyes. And the green leaves sticking to the black tar road reminded me of flags from an old parade. The air felt good, kind. *I* was feeling good. I tried to understand why, but only after a while did I figure it out: I hadn't quit.

Where the road turned inland, I saw someone walking toward me. For a small second I thought it was Bill Janick, and in spite of myself I stopped. The next moment I realized it was Terri. Just seeing her made me happy. I liked her.

When we got within thirty yards of one another I saw that she was carrying two cans of paint. She had to put them down every few yards because they were so heavy, wiggling her fingers to get the circulation back in her hands.

"Hi," was my greeting as I came up.

She wrinkled her nose as if there were some stink. "You look awful," she said.

"Thanks. I needed that."

"Are you all right?"

"Just sore."

"That's a real black eye," she said.

"I told you, I like polka dots. That the paint?"

She nodded. "And two brushes. I think there's more paint if you need it."

"I ran out of food again," I explained. "I was just

91

going to your store. We could leave the paint and stuff in the bushes and pick them up on the way back."

"Bill might be at the store," she warned.

Still feeling good, I shrugged. "Mr. Bermoldi said he won't do anything." Before she could object, I took the paint things and put them behind a tree where nobody could see them. "What colors did you get?"

"Red and orange."

"Fantastic."

Still she held back. "You sure you want to go?" she said.

"I have to eat, don't I?"

"I could bring you food."

"I want to get it," I insisted. "Come on."

Reluctantly she joined me. We walked along side by side, neither of us speaking. Without even looking, I knew her hand was swinging not more than a few inches from mine. I wondered if I should hold it. I mean, I wanted to, but didn't know how she would react.

We just walked.

But as we moved, I don't know, somehow our hands touched. I grabbed her hand. She gripped mine right away. We looked at each other and laughed.

"How's school?" I asked.

"The same," she said.

I don't know why, but that made us both laugh again.

We didn't say much about anything, but as soon as we came to the town center, in sight of the store, we let go of each other's hands and moved apart. We even walked slower. I began to wonder if Bill Janick would be there, and if it had been wise for me to come.

Terri went up the front steps first. "You coming?" she asked, seeing me hanging back. Understanding, she peered into the store window. "He's not here," she whispered and opened the door.

I followed.

The store was empty of customers. In the gray afternoon light it seemed gloomy, almost dingy. In the far corner, behind barred windows, Mrs. Janick was working on post office business, the rustling papers sounding like insects at work. Terri's sister, Pam, was mopping the floor behind the luncheonette counter. Her hair, in curlers, was tied up in a kerchief. Without makeup, her face seemed dry and dull.

When we walked in, both Terri's mother and sister stared at me.

"O my God," said Mrs. Janick in a whisper.

Pam said nothing, but after taking one long look, she bent over her mop and worked furiously.

For a time Mrs. Janick stayed behind her window, just watching me. I felt uncomfortable but didn't know what to do. Then she slowly came out and stood near the grocery counter, looking as if she had never seen anything like me in the world.

"That's terrible," she said, as much to herself as to me. "I'm sorry it happened. I'm even more sorry it was my son who did such a thing. We apologize." She sort of bowed her head.

I didn't know what to do. Pam, across the way, looked up. "Are you all right?" she asked.

"Sure," I said. "It's O.K."

Mrs. Janick continued to study my face. "Do your parents know?" she asked, her voice a nervous whisper.

"I, uh, wasn't going to tell them."

Mrs. Janick shook her head. "I want you to know we've punished Billy severely."

"Ed says Bill could go to jail for that," said Pam.

Mrs. Janick turned to look at me again. Embarrassed, I appealed to Terri. But she was behind me, eyes to the floor.

"Well," I said, feeling I had to say something, "I just wanted to get some things. I need some bread. Peanut butter. Milk."

"Yes, of course, of course," said Mrs. Janick, still unable to take her eyes from me. "Terri," she said, "get them, will you?" Moving quickly, she came out from behind the counter and headed out the back door.

Terri took her mother's place and slowly began to bring the things I wanted.

"Can I get you kids a soda?" offered Pam, breaking into the silence. "Pepsi? Sprite?"

"No thanks," I said.

"Come on. It's a treat," Pam said. "I promise it won't be poison. Not all of us are killers around here." Without waiting for a reply, she took two glasses and shoved them into the ice bin with a crunch, filling each two-thirds full. Then she set them under the soda faucet and turned the taps.

"Here they are," she said, sitting them on the counter.

I waited for Terri, who said, "She means it."

I really didn't want anything, but I sat down on one of the high stools. "Thanks," I said.

"Terri," said Pam. "You too."

Terri sat next to me.

Pam considered us for a moment. "It just goes to show," she said. "This island is *the* deadest place in the whole world. When something does happen, it's wrong. You'll see, they'll never put that hotel up."

I looked at Terri, realizing that she was looking past me, her eyes wide. I spun about, expecting the worst. Mr. Janick was standing by the back door, supporting himself with his crutches. For a moment, his small eyes seemed to point at me, then he shook his head.

"You were attacked," he said bluntly.

"I guess so," I replied, not knowing what else to say.

"Will your parents go to court?"

They all waited for me to answer, including Mrs. Janick, who had come back to peer over her husband's shoulder.

Before I could say anything, Mr. Janick said, "We punished him. Took away his car. Will you go to court?" he asked again.

I didn't know what to say. Instead, I kept thinking about what Bermoldi had said, that people were scared of me. I hadn't believed it then. But seeing how they were just waiting for me to answer, I knew it was true. I didn't like the feeling.

"No," I finally said. "I won't."

With a curt nod, Mr. Janick swung away, leaving me feeling stupid, as if *I* had done something wrong. But no sooner did he start to go, then he wheeled around sharply, so quickly his crutch struck the side of the wall with a hard crack. Face red with emotion, he shouted, "You provoked him! You did. We *need* that hotel! Go where you belong. Not here!" Spinning furiously about, he left the room, his crutches sounding like hammers on the floor. With a frightened look, Mrs. Janick scurried out after him.

I sat there numb.

"That was rotten," said Pam. "And Ed said you're being so decent." She picked up the mop, then seemed to think better about it and left Terri and me alone.

Neither of us could say anything.

Finally Terri slipped off the seat, got the rest of my groceries, and put them in a bag.

"How much is it?" I asked.

She shut her eyes and shook her head.

"Come on, Terri," I said. "I have to pay."

Again she shook her head.

I took out a bill and put it on the counter. "Terri, don't worry. I know you don't feel that way."

Slowly, she lifted her eyes and looked at me. There was nothing but pain on her face. "You don't understand, do you?"

I didn't want to hear any more. "Come on," I said. "We've got to get the paint."

By the time we reached the beach road the clouds had parted and the sinking sun was turning everything to a bright, awful pink. Down along the sand a whole bunch of seagulls were squabbling over a rotten fish, screaming at one another, jumping up and down like clowns.

That was pretty much the way I felt. All the way home we hadn't talked much. We gathered up the paint, and while she carried the groceries, I took the rest.

"You left your lights on," she said as the East Neck came into view.

I was sure I hadn't.

As we got closer, we saw that there was a car parked at the head of the driveway. As soon as we saw it, we stopped.

"Who does that car belong to?" I asked.

"It's not Bill's or Ed's," said Terri. "Is it your parents'?"

"One of these days they'll be here," I said. "But that's not them."

Walking again, I had this vague feeling that I had seen the car somewhere. Then I remembered. "It's Miss Devlin," I said.

Terri stopped walking.

"Come on," I said. "I need you."

She continued reluctantly.

The BMW was parked at the head of the driveway, like it didn't want to get any closer to the house than it had to. Even in the twilight, the car looked beautifully polished, bright and new.

"I don't see her," I said, looking all over, even by the bulldozer.

"I bet she's inside," suggested Terri. "It's her house."

The remark annoyed me, but I didn't say anything. I went in, getting Terri to move a little faster. We left the stuff in the kitchen.

Miss Devlin was standing in the middle of the main room, her back toward us when we came in. She wasn't dressed the way she had been the first time I saw her. Instead she had on slacks, boots, and a shiny blouse. Her hair was combed and hung down to the middle of her back.

"Hi," I said.

Surprised out of her concentration, she turned about, saw me, and frowned.

"Owen!" she said. "Ed Bermoldi told me what happened. I'm terribly sorry. Are you all right?"

"Sure," I said. "I'm O.K. This is Terri Janick, my friend."

"Hello, Terri," said Miss Devlin, but she kept her eyes on me. Then she turned back to the room. I had no idea what she was doing.

"Can I help you with something?" I said.

After a moment, she said, "Owen, when Ed told me what happened, I was very upset. It made me think that I hadn't been fair to you. I know you told me how strongly you felt about this place, but perhaps I didn't take it seriously enough. I apologize. Anyway, I decided I owed it to you to come and see for myself." She smiled warmly, then gazed about once more as if in search of something.

The way she spoke made me feel excited.

After some more long, silent looks, she slapped the side of her leg in an impatient gesture. "Owen, I've been here almost an hour. Do you know what I've decided?"

"No," I said, waiting for her to say what I wanted her to say.

"It's—ugly," she said. "I'm almost embarrassed to be so blunt. But really Owen, it has no—charm, no real character or strength. Nothing. I truly wish I could say otherwise. But I try to be an honest person. I know it means something to you. But I can't see one thing worth saving. Nothing. And certainly not when you put it into the balance with what could be here." She tried to smile.

Stunned is hardly the way I felt. If someone had slipped a straw inside of me and sucked out all my insides, that would have been closer.

She must have sensed what she had done. "I'm sure it has"—she fumbled around for words— "powerful and positive associations for you. Fond memories perhaps. But really, it's not worth saving. Consider what's at stake, Owen. I am sorry," she added with a little laugh. "I'm afraid I can't say more than that."

I just looked at her, hoping I wasn't showing what I was feeling. I even tried the half-smile. I don't think it worked.

"It'll happen on Saturday, Owen. Mr. Bermoldi requested that we do it as quickly as possible. I've told the construction company to do just that. No more waiting. We all agree. It's cruel to you. The earliest they can come is Saturday. It will be better for everybody, especially you."

It wasn't that I didn't want to say anything, I couldn't.

Miss Devlin looked past me, at Terri. "Are you one of the Janicks of Janick's General Store? 'All You'll Ever Need,' " she added with amusement, quoting from the sign over the store door.

"Yes, ma'am," Terri whispered.

"Terri, I wish you'd tell Owen how much this hotel means to the island. He won't believe me. I'm sure your brother will get work. It'll do fabulous wonders for your father's business. Your sister's fiancé will do well. Goodness knows, we'll have to have more policemen, and he's certain to be chief. And you can work here as much as you like during summers, perhaps after school. There always will be a need for good local people. Owen thinks I'm forcing this on all of you. Tell him I'm not. You want the hotel, don't you?"

I was certain that Terri would say she didn't want it, and I couldn't wait to see Miss Devlin's reaction. "Yeah," I said. "Tell us, Terri. Tell us what you think."

Miss Devlin insisted too. "The truth now. You want the hotel as much as everybody, don't you?"

For a moment we waited.

"Yes," said Terri softly, her eyes refusing to meet mine. "I do."

It may have been said softly, but I heard it. I might have been empty before. No longer.

"You see, Owen," said Miss Devlin. "Terri is no different from anyone else. I just wish I knew what you were thinking. Your generation tries to act so cool. When I was your age—and that's not so long ago, thank you—it was just the opposite. We were very emotional. Let it all hang out.

"Now," she said briskly, "if there is anything in this place that you want, by all means take it. I mean that. The place is yours. Do whatever you want with it. You don't even have to ask. From now till Saturday morning—I give it to you. Fair enough?"

I stood there, almost afraid of what was in me, afraid of my thoughts.

"Would you like to see the hotel plans?" she tried, bothered by my silence. "The architect's renderings for the new hotel are super. I brought them along for you to see. He's won all kinds of international awards. The plans are in my car." She looked at me. "I'm trying to show you how lovely and tasteful the new place will be."

"No thanks," I finally said.

She let out a long breath. "Well," she said, "I wish I could say I'm sorry. I *am* sorry for you, Owen, but not about the house. I like you. But this . . . is ugly." She held out her hand.

I just stood there.

She extended her hand for another moment, then gave up. "Isn't there anything you want to say? It's not healthy to bottle up your emotions, you know."

That tore it. I couldn't hold back. "Yeah," I said, "there is something I want to say."

She smiled with relief. "I wish you would say it then. You know I'm a good listener."

I looked her straight in the face. "I like ugly," I said slowly. "I hate everything you think is beautiful. I like ugly. *I love ugly!*"

The smile on her face stiffened. "You're very young after all," she said.

"You're a lot older than I thought too," I returned.

"But it does allow me to see that you're a spoiled, self-centered, and rude person. You don't intend to listen to anyone."

"And I suppose," I let her know, "that if I agreed with you, I'd be mature, social, and polite."

She thought of something else to say—I could see that—but gave it up. Instead she turned around and went out the back door. Terri and I stood where we were until we heard the car drive off.

I had had it. "I give up," I said. "I give up! I'm getting the hell out of here. Now! It was insane when it started, and it's gotten worse. The whole thing is a waste of time."

I tore into my room and started to throw my stuff into my suitcase.

"I mean there is nobody," I shouted at Terri, who had followed me to the door of the room, *"nobody* who thinks I'm right. You all want me to give up. My folks. That woman. Your brother. Your parents. The cop. Even you!" I shouted. "You really want them to put up that hotel, don't you? You really do. *Jobs?* You think you'll get all kinds of jobs, but you'll only be some kind of crummy waitress or some other piece of junk in a short skirt. Waiting on rich people. A servant to rich people. Cleaning up after them.

That's what you all do now! Admit it," I screamed at her. "That's all you'll ever want, to clean up after people!

"So what's the point?" I went on, slamming the suitcase lid and snapping the catches. "If it wasn't so stupid, it'd be funny." I was so angry, I lifted the suitcase up only to fling it down. The catches sprang open, and all my clothes poured out onto the floor.

Frantic, I grabbed all my things into one mass and tried to stuff it back. "Give me a hand, will you?" I called to Terri.

But when I looked up, Terri was gone.

Suddenly I realized what I had been saying. I ran out of the house. Sure enough, Terri was walking fast along the driveway.

"Hey, Terri," I called from the top of the back steps, "Hey, wait. I didn't mean that. Come on, Terri," I pleaded. She walked faster.

I jumped to the ground and started to run after her. "Hey, Terri," I shouted. "I apologize. I'm sorry. I didn't mean that. I was just angry. Terri!"

She whirled around. In the dark you could hardly see anything but those white eyes.

"You can always leave, can't you?" she cried out. "I can't. You won't listen to me any more than you will to anyone else. I'm trapped here. I thought you'd show me another way. But you can't. You just keep thinking of yourself!" Whirling around, she began to run down the road.

I started to run after her again, then stopped. "Please," I called after her. "Terri! Please!"

When I saw she wasn't going to stop, I watched her go. I stormed back to the house, angrier than ever. Or I started to. Instead I veered off down the beach. In my head, one word, "stupid," kept repeating itself over and over again.

At the high-water mark I stopped. The setting sun, ready to make its last plunge, seemed to get bigger and bigger. I had this feeling that I was seeing the sun for the first time for what it really was—a gigantic ball of fire.

"Ugly!" I cried out loud. "Ugly!" Then as loudly as I could, so loud that it hurt my throat, I screamed, *"I Love Ugly!"*

✳ A Memory of the Second Summer

Owen's father had taken him fishing. Mr. Coughlin had a long rod—new that year—and a large reel full of things that stuck out all over. It was black and silver, and six-year-old Owen thought it was wonderful.

Owen had a brand new dropline, a heavy green cord wrapped around a square of bright red dowels. A clumsy, heavy tear of lead, serving as sinker, was at the end. About a foot above the sinker Mr. Coughlin had fastened a hook that hung out like a long claw. Owen was afraid to touch it.

When Mr. Coughlin cast out his line, Owen dunked his line, which his father had baited, into the water and let the cord run until it bumped against the bottom.

After fishing for three hours Mr. Coughlin had caught twelve fish—eight porgies, three snappers, and a beautiful blue. Owen had caught nothing.

"Can't we go home?" Owen asked. They were out in the bay under the sun, and while he wore an upside-down sailor's hat, Owen felt hot, bored, and tired.

"You've got to be patient," his father said. "That's what fishing is all about."

Owen had had a few bites on his line. The first time he became so excited he almost lost the line. The second time he pulled in the line, but the bait—a hunk of clam—was gone. On the third bite Owen didn't do anything; he just let it stay in the water.

"I'm hungry," he tried, his eyes seeking the shore-line and the comfort of the house.

Mr. Coughlin reached into a bag and drew out some fig bars. "Help yourself," he offered.

Owen ate silently.

As he ate, he felt a sharp pull on his line. "Think I got a bite," he reported, not altogether sure.

Mr. Coughlin, instantly alert, swung about in the boat. "Don't move," he cautioned. "Let him come back."

Owen, forgetting his snack, waited breathlessly, his eyes fastened on the line that ran over the boat and deep down into the water.

There was another strike at the line, only this time there was no letup. The line began cutting circles in the water.

"I got it!" shouted Owen. "I got it!"

Hastily, Mr. Coughlin put down his own rod. "Now, Owen, wind it up slowly. Slowly!" He was pleased to see the excitement spread over his son's face.

Owen, pulling the fish in too fast, snarled the line, letting it drop off his spool so that it lay at his feet like a snare. He was so excited he could hardly hold on.

"I can't do it," he cried.

"Sure you can, Owen. Sure you can. Slowly, slowly," said Mr. Coughlin, who was becoming excited with his son's first catch. "Special dinner to-night," he announced.

Owen, holding on to the line with both small hands, peered into the water. Dimly he could see a brown fish dashing frantically below. "It's big! It's big!" he shouted.

With a sudden, nervous jerk, he pulled, and the fish all but flew into the boat. Landing on the bottom, it flopped about.

Owen looked at the fish, astounded. He had never seen such a fish. Even Mr. Coughlin was quiet.

"I'll be darned," said Mr. Coughlin. "A toadfish." He peered at it. "Now that's what I'd call ugly."

The fish had an enormous head, and in proportion, almost no tail at all. Without scales, it was covered with green slime. Its mouth, full of sharp teeth, was huge, and its fat, spitting lips sucked on the green line, all the while making grunting noises.

"What is it?" whispered Owen, horrified.

"Don't see many of those," said Mr. Coughlin. "Bottom feeders."

"I don't want it," said Owen. "It's ugly." He drew back.

The fish shook its stubby tail, opened and closed its huge mouth, gasping, making more grunting noises.

"Get it out!" Owen cried, suddenly feeling sick. "It's too ugly!"

He flung down the remains of his hopelessly snarled line and covered his eyes with his hands.

"It sure is," agreed Mr. Coughlin. "See that?" he said, pointing to two sharp fins. "Got poison in 'em."

"Get it out! Get it out!" cried Owen.

Mr. Coughlin put down his booted foot, squashing the top of the fish's head. With his hand he reached down and yanked out the fishhook, tearing the fish's mouth. There was blood. The fish grunted, gargled, struggled.

"Get it out! Get it out!" screamed Owen, now terrified.

Mr. Coughlin, himself upset, tried to pick up the fish, only to have it slip toward Owen. Owen scrambled away, became caught in his line, tripped over the seat. The boat began to sway.

Mr. Coughlin, suddenly fearful of capsizing the boat, roared, "Stay still!"

Owen froze.

Bending down, Mr. Coughlin trapped the fish in his hands and flung it into the water. Instantly, it vanished.

"Is it gone?" Owen asked, not daring to look.

Mr. Coughlin, feeling ill himself, said, "Yeah, it's gone. There was a gash on his finger, and his face was white. "Come here," he said, holding out a hand to his son.

Owen took it and flung himself on his father's shoulder, holding him tightly as the boat gently rocked. "I want to go home," he whimpered.

"Right," said Mr. Coughlin. "That's the best place, isn't it? Nothing ugly there."

Thursday

I didn't sleep very well. The bed was uncomfortable. There were times I felt cold. And I kept having dreams, really confusing dreams, though there seemed to be bits and pieces I knew, or faces I could almost but not quite recognize. For instance, I dreamed I was playing baseball with myself, nobody else, just myself. Or at least I couldn't see the people I was with. It was on the beach and the tide kept coming in and they kept calling me, telling me it was time to go. Only I didn't want to go because I was waiting to see a white bird. I *couldn't* leave. I was afraid to. I was waiting for something or someone to come back. Maybe it was Terri. I really couldn't tell what was going on.

None of it made any sense except that when I awoke in the morning, I felt more tired than when I went to sleep.

The room was full of bright sunshine. Automatically I reached for the blanket to pull over my head so that I could sleep some more. Then I remembered that I had no blanket. That's the kind of night it had been.

When the back door banged, I jumped. My first thought was that it was someone in the kitchen: Terri. I went to have a look, fast. The moment I got there

I was met by another bang of the busted back door. It wasn't anyone at all. Disappointed, I pulled the door shut tight.

I took the milk from the fridge and drained it off, milk dribbling down my chin and neck.

In the bathroom I studied my face in the mirror. The bruises had turned different shades of purple, but the lump on my forehead had gone down a lot. My lip was no longer puffy.

For breakfast I had mushroom soup cooked in the tuna can, along with lumps of peanut butter served on fingers. It made me feel a little sick, but I told myself that there was no going back to Janick's.

The main thing was that I knew what I had to do.

I changed my clothes and brought out the paint cans and brushes. Opening the cans was a bit of a problem until I remembered the thingamajig for the propane tanks that was in with the plastic spoons. It worked fine.

I started painting the windows first. Red, all red. I don't mean *around* the glass, but the entire window, glass and all. Everything red. When I was done, each window would be a great red square.

When I finished the first window, I stepped back to see how it looked. I have to admit it looked strange. Still, I had no intention of stopping.

As it turned out, it took much longer and was harder to do than I thought it would be, but by midday I had all the windows painted red.

I walked back along the driveway, past the bulldozer, to see how the house looked. It was bizarre. The red windows made the house look like there was a fire inside. I thought it was great.

Inside the house it looked even stranger. The rooms glowed with a look of fire, as if I had stepped right into the middle of the sun I had seen the night before.

Back on the driveway, I took a long look at the house, trying to decide what to do next. From time to time I looked at the bulldozer, thinking of painting that too. But I didn't even want to touch it. I concentrated on the house.

I took up the orange paint and with the smaller brush began to work. I painted stars, five-pointed stars, solid orange, on the sides of the house. As I painted, the star points began to run.

I stepped back to see what I had done. It looked like stars flying through the air, the paint drips seeming like cartoon marks. I thought it was fantastic.

Not caring any longer if they dripped, I painted even more stars. In a few places the orange slipped over and across the red windows.

I liked that too.

Bit by bit I began to get a sense of what I was painting—a picture of the universe, *my* universe, the way I wanted things to be.

Painting the stars took the rest of the day. My only worry was that I wouldn't have enough paint to put on as many stars as I wanted. Sure enough, by late afternoon I ran out of paint.

I made up my mind fast. I took the rest of the money—about twenty-five bucks—and went as fast as I could across the island to the ferry landing, the island's downtown. Near the landing was a hardware store where I could buy paint.

White paint was the cheapest, so I decided to buy that, two large cans of it, as much as I could afford. I hurried back, hoping to reach the house before dark. But it was too late to work any more that day.

I felt good. After a long time I was doing something, the right thing.

I ate some more soup. When I slept that night, I didn't have dreams. I wasn't dreading the last days anymore.

☀ A Memory of the Fourth Summer

"Well, Owen," said his mother as she tucked her eight-year-old son into bed and sat down beside him, "tomorrow's the last day of summer. What are we going to do?"

"Where are we going?" he asked.

"You know perfectly well. Pittsburgh. We visited before we came here. You even picked out your room. And you'll like it, you know you will. They say it's a nice school. So we do have to go, don't we?"

"I guess."

"What are you going to do tomorrow then?"

"I don't know yet."

"Well," she said, kissing his forehead, "think about it. It should be something special. You decide." Turning out the light, she left the room.

Owen, wide awake in the dark, tried hard to think what he would do. There were so many things. They could have a cookout. They could go sailing. They could go fishing or swimming. They could just lie on the beach. All the things they always did, all the things they liked to do.

He wished he didn't have to go to a new place, wished he didn't have to go to a new school. Why couldn't they just stay here? It was such a long time before the next summer, and he hadn't done everything he had wanted to do.

What could he do tomorrow—the last day?

Somewhere in the middle of his thoughts he drifted off into sleep, only to wake up a few hours later. He didn't even know he had slept.

He listened. Everything was quiet, quieter than normal. He began to wonder what time it was.

He got up, swinging his feet to the cool floor. The sound of his brother's sleepy breathing drifted across the room.

Carefully he made his way out of their room only to stand in the middle of the main room. Completely quiet. In the faint moonlight, the room, walled in by shadows, seemed small and pressed in on him.

He moved through the front porch where his sister was sleeping and then outside. He sat down on the front steps and looked up at the stars. There were always more stars over the East Neck than in cities. In cities you could almost count the stars. On the East Neck you couldn't even begin.

So quiet.

Restless, wide awake, Owen walked down the beach to the water. There he wiggled his toes in the soft surf, letting it wash back and forth over him. Hitching up his pajamas, he waded in, ankle deep.

What, he wondered, would it be like to swim in the dark?

What, he wondered, would he do tomorrow, the last day?

What, he wondered, would he do over all the time before they came back next year?

The water felt warm, the air cool.

Standing there, he began to know what he wanted to do on the last day. He would make a list, the long-

III

est list in the whole world, pages and pages and pages—and on it would be all the things he would do when they came back next summer.

The last day would be next year's first day.

Friday

As soon as there was enough light I was up on the roof. There I painted great puffballs of clouds with the new white paint. Before long, the entire area was my notion of a summer day.

Not that I was satisfied. Remembering what Terri had said about getting paint from the boat yard, I went there myself. I didn't see anyone about till I went through the boat sheds. There I found someone calking a boat.

"Help you?" he asked.

"I'm looking for some paint," I told him.

He examined me carefully. "You the East Neck kid?"

"I guess so." It was weird to be known that way.

"You'll have to go down to the hardware store for paint," he said, turning his back on me and going on with his work.

I stood there for a moment. "Aren't there any partly empty cans about?" I asked. "I don't have any money. And I don't care what kind of paint it is."

He continued his work a while longer, then abruptly got up. Motioning to me to follow, he led me behind a large shed to a place where garbage was piled.

"Root around here," he said. "You might find

something. It's summer people's leavings." Without another word, he left.

I knew he had been trying to insult me, but I didn't care. As soon as he left I searched and found a can of black paint, one of green, and best of all, one of silver.

I took all three cans.

On the way back I tried to make up my mind what to do next, and by the time I got to the house I knew.

There were the red sun windows. There were the streaking orange stars. There was the white cloud roof. I started on the chimney, painting that black, hoping it looked something like a tree. To help, I ran out some branch lines from the main chimney "trunk," both on the roof and along the sides of the house. Then, with the green paint, I laid on some leaves. Not too much like a tree, but good enough for me.

The silver paint was something else. It took me a long time to decide how to use that. There wasn't much of it; it had to be for something special. I thought of things like a gigantic silver bird and a sailboat flying through my universe.

I didn't do either of those things.

I climbed the roof, and writing in huge letters with the silver paint, I wrote one word over everything:

BEAUTIFUL!

That evening I went back on top of the dune, the exact place where I had hidden when my parents had left, to look over what I had done. It didn't take me long to decide that the house *was* beautiful—alive, sparkling, and glowing, even to the silver letters catching the sun's sinking light. Nothing I had ever done made me feel so good.

I stood there, hands in back pockets, feeling great, liking it and me.

Fact is, I was concentrating so much on the house and the way the red color changed as the sun went down that I didn't notice a car pull up in the driveway behind where I was standing.

When I realized someone was there, I turned around fast.

It was my parents.

I was so surprised that I just looked at them. It occurred to me that I could run, but at the same time I realized I didn't have to.

As soon as the car stopped, my father jumped out and shouted, "Owen!" as if I were going someplace.

My mom got out of the car too. They were both dressed in their city clothes.

They stared at me. "You all right?" was the first thing my mother called to me.

I stood there, not saying anything, realizing that they were looking hard at me, trying to see what kind of shape *I* was in. They hadn't really seen the house. Watching to see their reaction when they did, I could only grin.

But they didn't see it. They kept looking at me.

"Officer Bermoldi called us every night," my father said. "Said we weren't to worry about you, that he had everything under control. That's why we didn't come sooner. He told us you had a scuffle with some kids. But it looks much worse than that."

"I'm O.K.," I said.

"O.K.?" my mother repeated in horror. "You look dreadful. Are you ready to come home now?"

"Hey, look over there," I said, pointing to the house.

They turned and for the first time saw the house. For a moment they just gaped at it, then my father swung back to look at me, then at the house again. Mom, after looking at it, just stared at me.

"Did you do that?" she finally asked.

I nodded, grinning.

She turned back to the house again. It surprised me how nervous I was, how I needed to know what they thought, how I wanted them to like it. But they said nothing.

"What do you think?" I had to ask.

My father squinted up at me. "I don't think you should have done that," he said. "The place doesn't belong to you."

"Come on," I said. "Tell me what you think of it."

"Well," my father tried, staring at the house, then at me again. "I can tell you one thing; I never saw anything like it before."

"Why," my mom asked, "did you write 'beautiful!' on the roof like that?"

"Like the title on a book," I said.

Again they stared at it. And again I had to ask, "Like it?"

"You sure you had permission?" Dad asked. "I mean, people are going to think you're crazy."

"Maybe I am."

"It's original," Mom tried.

"Do you like it!" I shouted.

"Will you please come down here," was my father's response. "We're concerned about *you,* not about the house."

"Not till you tell me what you think," I said. But

116

at the same time I saw that it made no sense to them at all.

My father seemed to understand that himself. "Give us a break, Owen. I don't know what to say. I'll have to think about it. Please come down."

Giving up, I walked down the dune. My father held his hand out to me, but I had no intention of getting any closer. Hands in pockets, I stood off.

"When's the demolition?" my father asked.

"Tomorrow supposedly," I said.

"Why spend all that time on the house if you know it's coming down?" my mother wanted to know.

"Dressing up for the funeral," I said, putting on my half-smile.

Shaking her head, she walked toward the house. "Your high school called us," she said as she went.

"What did you tell them?" I wanted to know.

My father seemed a little embarrassed. "We couldn't very well tell them you were sulking over the loss of a summer cottage, could we? We said you were sick."

My mother stood on the rear steps of the house. "What have you been eating?" she called.

"Enough," I told her.

My father became impatient. "Come on," he said. "Go get your stuff. We're leaving."

I backed off. "I told you. I'm not going." This time I was ready to run. There was no way I was going to end the whole thing now.

"Owen, what's the point?" my father asked. He really was tired. It had been a long day for both of them. They must have left right after work.

"Haven't you done enough?" my mother joined in. "It's not a joke. Everybody's upset. You've already had one unpleasant experience. We've rented rooms at the Grenlow Inn for tonight. I think you could use a good meal. We'll go home tomorrow."

I shook my head. "I want to see if they really take it down," I said.

"Of course they will," my father said slowly. "There's absolutely no one who wants to keep this place."

"I do."

"Owen," he said, "do you really expect the whole world to head off in another direction because you're stuck on this place? Beautiful!" He shook his head. "You're wrong. It isn't. What's more, it never was. Do you know why *we* got this house? Because no one else wanted it. And you've only made it worse, into some"—he searched desperately for a word—"into a joke."

My mother put a hand on his arm, trying to restrain him. He wasn't to be stopped.

"You think," he continued, "that you can do anything you want. You can't. I can't. Nor can your mother or your brother or your sister. Or anybody for that matter. Wanting hasn't anything to do with what happens. All you've done is paint yourself a—a thing—a monument to three weeks of the year. What about the rest of the year? Kid stuff! And it's about time you understood that. Now get into the car and let's get out of here. I'm sick and tired of this."

"Please," my mother pleaded, "do as he says, Owen."

"I'm not going," I said.

I looked at my father. I had never seen him that way before. His face was dead gray, his fingers jumpy. I didn't know if he was going to hit me or burst into tears. He started to say something, then didn't. Instead he turned about and went to the car, leaned on it, his back toward me.

"What time is the house going to come down?" asked my mother, exhausted.

"It's *not* coming down," I said.

She shook her head. "Owen, Mr. Bermoldi promised us it would be early tomorrow morning."

"It's not coming down!" I yelled.

She looked at my father, at the house, at me. "If you change your mind, we'll be at the inn. Otherwise we'll be back for you in the morning."

I didn't say anything.

She started to pass by me, then stopped to take my arm. "Do you know what I think the difference is between kids and grown-ups?"

I looked at her.

She said, "Grown-ups know when to forget. Kids don't. Kids won't let go."

When they drove off, there it was again. Nobody but me, the house, and the bulldozer. Like square one again. But it wasn't, not really.

We were almost at the end.

Countdown time.

The truth of the matter was I still wasn't sure what I was going to do. I just didn't know.

My first decision was to stay up all night. Just the thought of it made me hungry, so I ate what I had been eating all along, hating it more and more.

Night came. I remembered that mornings on the island were like the day before the world began. This night was like the day after the world ended. No stars, no sounds. Nothing. Wrapped in nothing.

I decided to put on all the house lights, go outside, and see what it looked like. To my eyes it was a spectacular success, the windows bursting with the look of real sunfire, the sun I had made.

Something real.

Inside the house again, I began to pace, knowing I was bored, tense, only waiting for the morning to happen, wishing it wouldn't come, trying again and again to figure out what to do.

If I had one real wish, it was that Terri would come. I even went to the telephone to check if in some fashion it could be gotten to work again.

Lifeless—not even static.

I made myself push Terri out of my mind.

Instead I thought about what my parents had been saying when they were leaving. I wasn't mad at them, not really. Just sorry. They couldn't understand what I was doing. I knew I was upsetting them, making them feel bad. I *was* sorry about that. I just didn't know how else to act.

I wasn't like them, that's all. And if being an adult was doing what my mother said—learning how to forget—well, I couldn't. I just couldn't. And I swore I wouldn't.

In spite of myself I thought about the Janicks, the whole family, about how they all made me feel uncomfortable. I didn't like them—except for Terri. The others were small, creepy. They wanted people to feel sorry for them. I was glad I wouldn't have to see them again.

Mr. Bermoldi, of all the people, I thought had been honest. Then again, I wasn't so sure. He would be made police chief. He was playing up to everyone. Well, why not? Didn't they all want things to change?

I didn't.

Miss Devlin. Just thinking about her made me furious. She was the cause of it all, the biggest liar in the lot. In spite of what she said, she was only doing it—I was sure—for the money.

I hated them all, wishing there was some way I could show them what I thought.

At exactly eleven o'clock, without any warning, the lights went off.

My first thought was that Bill Janick and his friends were coming back to get their last licks, and I was scared. I stood in the middle of the main room listening for some sound, any sound, to tell me something.

I heard nothing.

Cautiously I went outside. Only then did I figure out what had happened. The electrical power had been cut off in readiness for the demolition. They couldn't very well knock down a house with the electricity still on.

Once outside I stayed out, straying toward the beach, even considering the possibility of a last swim. That, I didn't have to remind myself, was really crazy. Too dark.

I strolled down to the water's edge, hearing no sound but that of my own feet on the sand. After a while I stopped and glanced back. To my astonishment the house was gone. It had vanished in the dark. It was nowhere, and for the moment, so was I.

I stood there, frightened, thinking I would never be able to find my way.

I ran as fast as I could, back along the beach, until I saw it. But what I saw was only an empty hole in the dark, as if the night had a hard, black pit. For a moment I felt so alone. But standing there I made myself refuse to see it that way. I forced myself to see the house as it truly was.

And I could see it. For I remembered so much that the house became alive with the light of many days.

It was then that I made the most important discovery of all. The house had become a memory. I had been looking at what I remembered, not anything real. My head was seeing it, not my eyes. And it had been that way ever since I was told the house would have to go.

When I understood this, I finally understood why I loved the place so much. It was because of all the memories, memories that each year promised me summers yet to come. The house was the place—for me—where everything began again and again and again. Having that place, that past, gave me a future. The house had given me that much.

And I? What could I do for the house? I couldn't keep it, hold it, save it. Everybody wanted it to go. Everybody but me.

Maybe I had been wrong—wrong to my parents, wrong to the island people, wrong to Terri, wrong to keep them from the summers *they* so desperately wanted, needed, had to have. They didn't have my memories. To get them, they had to take the house away, put it aside, bury it under the promise of the hotel. Maybe they did need that. Maybe it was their only hope.

I didn't have to hope. The place had taught me that summers would come. Each one different. But summers would still come. They always had, they always would.

At last I knew what I had to do. The house had to come down. For them. But *nobody* had the right to take it down but me. Because only I could remember what it was. Remembering was the thing I could give. Remembering was my kind of love.

So I stood there—holding on to my memories, my love for that house. It was what I had been, and was, and ever could be. Me. A place they called ugly.

My memories knew better. The house was beautiful. And maybe, just maybe, so was I.

I made my way back to the house and got into bed. As I lay there, how full the house was. How full was I! "You're not dead!" I kept telling the house. "I'll remember you. That way you won't ever be dead. I won't let *them* do it. I'll do it. And I'll make them remember too. *I promise!*"

Saturday

It was about seven o'clock in the morning when I awoke, right away worried that I had overslept. As dark as it had been when I had fallen asleep, now it was bright enough to make me blink.

The first thing I did was go outside and scout around. I didn't see anyone. I ran to the top of the dune and looked down on the bulldozer. It was there, as motionless as ever.

I considered using it to do the job. I was sure I could drive it. But the bulldozer was *their* way, not mine. My way would be better.

I got everything ready.

Inside the house, I shoved all my stuff into my suitcase, mixing clean and unclean things. I didn't care. That done, I took the suitcase out of the house and hid it behind a clump of marsh grass.

Then I waited for them to make their move.

The first person to arrive was Bermoldi. His police car pulled up to the top of the driveway and sat there. He couldn't see me, but from where I was on the screened-in porch, I could see him. He remained motionless, looking over the house. I really would have loved to have known what was in his mind. The only clue he gave was a shake of his head. Then he got out and marched into the house the back way.

"Owen?" he called.

I went to meet him.

"Hi," he said. "How're you doing?"

I shrugged. "O.K."

"You look a lot better. You speak to your folks?"

"Yeah," I said, no longer surprised that he knew everything that was going on. "You know where they are."

"Right," he said, a slight smile on his face. "Hey, today's the day. In fact, this morning."

"If you say so."

He lifted his hands as if he were praying. "We going to have any problems?"

"What do you mean?"

"Owen," he said, his patience straining, "they are coming to knock the place down."

"Maybe they won't."

He laughed in a phony way. "O.K. Game time. *If* they come, do you intend to be in here?"

I studied his face, knowing that there was no way I was even going to hint at what I was going to do.

Before I could answer, he said, "Because I'll tell you right now, I won't let you stay. I'll haul you out myself. I've no intention of letting you kill yourself. But if you come out on your own, then we'll all be cool. You can walk your own steps."

"As long as I get out."

"Right."

It felt like he was offering terms of surrender.

"There's no way they'll take it down," I said.

"*If* they do, Owen . . ." He let the sentence dangle.

"I'm not going to let myself get killed, if that's what you're worried about," I told him.

He smiled. "Good enough. Now, Owen baby, it's your show. And hey," he said, smiling, "I like what you did with the house. I'll hate to see it—and you—go."

"I'll come back when you've been made police chief," I said.

His smile vanished. "Sure, kid. We'll have a party—out on the beach." And he went out.

I returned to the porch and watched through the screen. The countdown was still on, and I was beginning to feel sick.

Plumbers came. I hadn't expected that, and I really got worried. They came in a red truck, two guys I had never seen before. After speaking briefly with Bermoldi, they carried huge wrenches and went to the wellhead where they began to work at cutting off the water.

It was like a siege. I wondered who would give in first.

One of the plumbers even walked into the house and turned on the kitchen tap. He paid no attention to me. The tap spattered, blew out water, gave a gurgle, then trickled down to nothing. Satisfied, the man left, taking the telephone with him.

I felt a lot better when the plumbers had gone.

My parents were the next to come. They drove right up behind Bermoldi's car. It was like Bermoldi was the general-in-chief of the siege. No one could get in their shots without his permission.

What really annoyed me was watching my father give Bermoldi money. I didn't know if he was paying him back the money Bermoldi had given me or something else. Like paying him off.

My mother came into the kitchen.

I refused to go out to meet her.

"Owen," she called. "Where are you?"

"Here," I replied from the rocker in the main room.

She came in and looked at me. "Can we leave now?" she asked.

"I told you when I'd go," I said.

"Well," she tried, "they are—"

"They won't," I cut in.

She was really worried. "We'll be outside. Where's your suitcase? At least I can take that."

"Don't worry about it."

"Did you have breakfast? Why are the windows all shut? What do you intend to do?"

"Leave me alone!" I shouted at her. She was making me even more nervous than I already was.

Fortunately, she retreated.

About half an hour later, Terri arrived. I was sitting on the porch when she came. As soon as I saw who it was, I stood up. She was the only one I wanted to come into the house. But she was the only one, so far, who didn't come in. Instead she kept her distance out on the road, arms crossed, just looking.

Watching her made me go through what felt like fifty feelings all at once, from anger to I don't know what. I mean, she had tried to be straight with me. I knew that now. I hadn't wanted to listen to her, no more than to anyone else. And I wanted so much to know what she was thinking, wondering if she thought the house was beautiful.

She didn't give a sign. Just stared. I knew then that I had treated her the worst of anyone. And I would never see her again.

Soon after, Miss Devlin came, dressed in a business suit. It figured.

As she jumped out of her car and looked at the house I watched her closely, getting a kick out of her surprise. She went back into her car and pulled out a camera.

That made me furious.

There was nothing I could do as she leaned against that fancy car of hers and took pictures. I couldn't help thinking how the house was good enough for her to keep in pictures, but not good enough for her to keep for real.

Even so, for the moment, my hopes began to rise again. If she *was* taking pictures, if she really thought what I had done was special, maybe there was a last possibility that she would change her mind. I had this sudden vision of her ordering a crane and picking up the whole house and moving it, with me inside, to some other spot.

But when she was finished with the camera, she put it away, went over to my parents, shook hands with them, and began to talk. They stopped looking at the house.

It was going to happen. No way out. I didn't know who I hated more, Miss Devlin or myself, for what I had to do. But it had to be soon. I couldn't take much more.

Finally, a man drove up in a car, an old Plymouth Valiant, drab olive green, like an army reject. At first I wasn't sure who the guy was. When he came out of the car wearing a bright yellow hardhat, I knew. A helmet. A siege. The official executioner.

The man spoke to Bermoldi, then to Miss Devlin, who introduced him—I don't know why—to my parents. Then they all kept looking at the house, talking about it. But pretty soon the group broke up, and Bermoldi walked down the driveway and into the house.

"Owen!"

I showed myself. And I noticed how edgy he was. I wondered if he had any idea what was going to happen.

"This is it," he said.

"Going to smash it down?" I said.

"Going to smash it down," he returned.

"For real?"

"Real as rock."

"So everybody can live happily ever after?"

"Something like that," he said.

We looked at each other. He was leaning slightly back on his heels, hands on his hips, stomach bulging out over his heavy, bullet-filled belt. And me, I was just standing there, feet wide, hands in my back pockets with nothing much else but my half-smile and my sunglasses, wondering who was the winner, him or me.

"Do you want me to say you put up a good fight?" he offered with an edge to his voice that hadn't been there before.

"Maybe I haven't finished," I said. "Do I hold my hands over my head when I come out?"

He grinned. "All the honors of war."

"Where do I stack my guns?"

"By the corral."

I gave him the one eyebrow. I think it worked.

"Hey, come on, buddy," he said. "Give. Admit it. You lose. We win." Turning on his heel, he went out.

Right then I knew that *I* was going to win.

After a moment, my heart beating like crazy, I got ready to move out. In my mind I kept telling myself: "Remember. . . . Remember. . . ."

On the last morning, right after Owen got up, he went to the drawer where the plastic picnic spoons were and took out the special tool for the propane gas tank. Then he went outside, and remembering what he had been taught long ago by Mr. Hinks, he turned off the valve of the remaining tank.

With the other end of the tool he unlocked the tank from its mounting and began to drag it around the house, up the back steps, and into the house, and finally into the main room. Carefully he placed it on the floor behind the wicker rocker, checking to see if anyone could see it. When he was sure they wouldn't be able to, he left it where it was. That done, he went around the house and made sure all the windows were tightly closed.

From the kitchen he got one of the empty peanut butter jars and after loosely stuffing newspaper into it, screwed the top back on. With a nail he punched three holes into the lid.

He put the jar outside, behind the clump of marsh grass where he had hidden his suitcase.

After that it was merely a question of waiting, all the while telling himself that if he didn't do it, they would. And only he had the right.

Then the people came. When Bermoldi left for the second time, Owen knew that it was time to act.

Heart going like crazy, he gripped the steel tool for the propane tank, amazed to find it slippery. Then he saw it was sweat from his hand and wiped it dry on his jeans.

He looked outside. They were waiting, all of them, looking for him to come out, to give up.

He had to close his eyes for a moment, thinking he was going to be sick. One small corner of his eyelid fluttered. He had no control over it.

"I won't forget," he said out loud. "I won't." Reaching for the propane tank that lay on the floor in the main room, Owen fastened the tool over the valve and twisted it.

The hissing gas rushed into the room.

Owen ran for the back door.

Closing the door tightly behind him, he hurried to the spot where he had hidden his suitcase and the newspaper-stuffed peanut butter jar.

Turning, he faced the house.

The others were standing in a great circle. In the middle was the house, its orange stars cutting through red suns and white clouds, the black and green chimney tree. Over this universe—his universe—in great silver letters—one word:

BEAUTIFUL!

A loud, hacking cough made them all look around. The bulldozer had started, shooting up a shot of filthy smoke from its exhaust pipe.

Fumbling as he rushed, Owen yanked his father's butane lighter from his pocket. He unscrewed the lid from the peanut butter jar, turned it upside down, then lit the paper, holding the jar as the paper burned and smoldered.

"Stand away!" he yelled. "Keep away!"

The people looked up, puzzled. Bermoldi stared at Owen, trying to understand.

"Keep away!" Owen screamed.

He screwed the top back on the jar. Air, sucked in through the holes, fed the fire.

Bermoldi acted. Leaping from his place by the car, he began pushing people back.

The bulldozer—huge, hard, and yellow—started to come around the sand dune. Its blade, red with rust, was high off the ground. To Owen's eyes it looked like a warrior's shield—a warrior coming in for the kill.

Bermoldi rushed toward the driver, waving his arms and yelling. The driver heard him and flipped the ignition key, bringing the machine to a dead stop. He all but dove off, scurrying behind the cars with the other people.

Looking frantically about to see that everybody was back far enough, Owen, trembling now, took the jar, hot and buzzing with the fire it contained, and threw it at the nearest window.

There was a crash of glass.

Instantly, silently, the house began to swell, like some great ungainly balloon of wood. The walls began to pry apart. The roof rose a few feet into the air. Through every widening crack a red glare could be seen, hot, burning, expanding.

And then, just as quickly, the house collapsed, only to be followed by the sounds of a short, sharp explosion, a sucking wind, a tearing of wood.

In three seconds it was over, leaving nothing but a dull thud in Owen's ears.

As the flames licked and spat over the rubble of the house a dirty white feather of smoke tried to rise and fly. Then it too vanished.

All that remained was a silence broken by the mindless, endless lapping of bay waves.

Owen looked about. From behind their cars people

were staring out at him. He picked up his suitcase and walked toward his parents' car.

No one spoke.

"That part was for you to remember," he managed to say. "I'll remember the rest."

When he got into the car and started to move away, he began to cry, cried for the summers that were—and for the summers yet to come.

Avi has written nearly thirty books for young readers, including the Newbery Honor books *The True Confessions of Charlotte Doyle* and *Nothing But the Truth.* His other titles cover a remarkably wide range of genres, from adventures to historical fiction to dramatic coming-of-age stories. When he's not writing, Avi travels all over the United States, speaking and giving readings of his books at schools and conferences. A former librarian, he currently lives in Denver, Colorado, with his wife.

Look for All the Unforgettable Stories by Newbery Honor Author

★AVI★

THE MAN WHO WAS POE 71192-3/ $4.99 US/ $6.99 Can

NOTHING BUT THE TRUTH 71907-X/ $4.99 US/ $6.99 Can
(NEWBERY HONOR)

A PLACE CALLED UGLY 72423-5/ $4.99 US/ $6.99 Can

SOMETHING UPSTAIRS 70853-1/ $4.99 US/ $6.50 Can

SOMETIMES I THINK I HEAR MY NAME
72424-3/$4.50 US/ $6.50 Can

THE TRUE CONFESSIONS OF CHARLOTTE DOYLE
(NEWBERY HONOR) 71475-2/ $4.99 US/ $6.99 Can

PUNCH WITH JUDY 72253-4/ $4.50 US/ $5.99 Can

Thought-Provoking Novels from Today's Headlines

HOMETOWN
by Marsha Qualey   72921-0/$3.99 US/$4.99 Can

Border Baker isn't happy about moving to his father's rural Minnesota hometown, where they haven't forgotten that Border's father fled to Canada rather than serve in Vietnam. Now, as a new generation is bound for the Persian Gulf, the town wonders about the son of a draft dodger.

NOTHING BUT THE TRUTH
by Avi   71907-X/$4.99 US /$6.99 Can

Philip was just humming along with *The Star Spangled Banner*, played each day in his homeroom. How could this minor incident turn into a major national scandal?

THE HATE CRIME
by Phyllis Karas   78214-6/$3.99 US/$4.99 Can

Zack's dad is the district attorney, so Zack hears about all kinds of terrible crimes. The latest case is about graffiti defacing the local temple. But it's only when Zack tries to get to the bottom of this senseless act that he fully understands the terror these vicious scrawls evoke.

Avon Flare Presents
Powerful Novels
from Award-winning Authors

Joyce Carol Thomas

Bright Shadow   84509-1/$4.99 US/$6.99 Can
Marked by Fire   79327-X/$4.50 US/$6.50 Can

Alice Childress

A Hero Ain't Nothing But a Sandwich
                       00312-2/$4.50 US/$5.99 Can
Rainbow Jordan   58974-5/$4.50 US/$5.99 Can

Virginia Hamilton

Sweet Whispers, Brother Rush
                       65193-9/$4.99 US/$6.99 Can

Theodore Taylor

The Cay   01003-8/$4.99 US/$6.50 Can
Sniper   71193-1/$4.99 US/$6.50 Can
The Weirdo   72017-5/$4.50 US/$6.50 Can
Timothy of the Cay   72119-8/$4.50 US/$5.99 Can